While the Rain Whispered

Letters to Layton
Book Three

Kim Williams

For my Daddy, Jerry White.
In memory of my father-in-law, Ray Williams.

While the Rain Whispered

Her mind drifted to the first time Papa had hoisted her atop his shoulders and galloped around the yard when the butterflies danced. She'd not known such joy existed.

Chapter 1

MAY 1937 | LAYTON, TEXAS

Life is simply one generation fading while another takes its first breath. Clara stood alone in the middle of the church graveyard where her best friend, elegant Mary Forder, buried her father moments ago. Clara sighed. The decisions and adventures between beginning and end determine how one person impacts another. Thus far her life was well-guided and cared for, but contentment escaped her. Her heart was encumbered with longing for something she couldn't identify, and most likely couldn't obtain. Why was she not content with life in her rural East Texas town of Layton, especially when her family had survived the worst of the Great Depression? The question shamed her.

A warm May breeze blew her russet curls across the pale brown angel kiss on her cheek. She reached up, touched it, then smiled. *Momma says the mark makes me special. I don't feel special.*

Wallace James, the young man who owned her heart, or more accurately, desired to own her heart, approached her. His spicy scent announced him.

Clara looked up to meet his gaze and released tears created by a complexity of emotions. His affection for her apparent in his eyes as they swept over her face. He handed her a handkerchief then spoke above a whisper.

"Clara, are you thinking about Mary?"

She looked away realizing her thoughts had been on herself.

She sniffled, then wiped tears from her cheeks. "I was thinking about life and death and all that's in between. But I do wonder how one bears the pain of a father dying."

Wallace touched her shoulder. "I reckon it's grace. God gives you the grace to bear it just when you need it."

His faith had been strong for as long as she'd known him. *Him almost a teenager. Her a sassy little girl.*

Clara reached and took his hand, then drew in a shallow breath at her impulse. A warmth surged through her at the contact. Her fingers drew

1

together as Wallace squeezed her hand. His tug was gentle, and she found her cheek against his coat. Her back secured by his arm. Wallace's chin rested against her hair. Her five-four thin body was engulfed in his six-four stature.

"Don't worry over your Papa, Clara. I suspect he has a lot of years ahead of him."

Wallace felt strong against her thin frame.

And just as quickly as he'd pulled her to him, she felt him release his hold and her grip.

"Your Papa sent for you. It's time to leave for lunch at the Forder's house."

Wallace had six more years experience at life than her nearly eighteen. Had he found contentment?

"Are you happy, Wallace?"

He slanted his head.

"I know you're sad this moment, but I mean all in all, are you happy?"

His fingers moved up and down his chin.

"Yes. I have things others long to have. A job. A place to live, even if it is the side room of the garage where I work." He tweaked her nose. "A good family. Good friends. Your family being some of them."

"You don't want for something more than that?"

His face reddened.

Clara often spoke from impulse. It was a trait she didn't like about herself. Too often she regretted her words while speaking them. This was one of those moments. She'd opened the door to the one uneasiness between them.

"There is something I want so bad it consumes my thoughts. But I've learned to wait."

She gentled her huff just as it released.

Clara suspected Wallace was in love with her and wished to marry her. She also suspected her huff disappointed him, for she watched his jaw twitch before he formed a grin.

"Your angel kiss is beautiful." Her traitorous insides quivered as he lifted thick fingers toward her mark on her cheek, but pulled back and stuffed his hand in a coat pocket.

"It embarrasses me."

"It shouldn't. I cherish it."

2

"Cherish?"

His lips spread and reached high cheekbones. "Yes. Cherish."

"Wallace, people don't cherish birthmarks. They like them, dislike them, or care less, but they don't cherish them."

"I cherish your mark because I cherish you, young lady."

"Wallace, that's dumb. You can't cherish me. You're not my father or even my brother." Clara hoisted her hands to her hips.

"And I thank God for that every day."

Wallace's tone sounded brotherly, although she assumed he was attempting to mask his romantic affection this time.

Clara could admit that she loved Wallace, in a big brother sort of way, and couldn't imagine her life without his friendship. So he did own her heart as a friend, but nothing more at the time. After all, she wanted more from life than the familiar. Her children's stories had more adventure in them than her own story.

He motioned her forward with his head. "Family's waiting on you."

"Are you coming to the Forders?"

"No. I've got to return to the garage. Seeing it isn't a Forder owned business I didn't close it for the day."

Wallace had grown up on a farm the next town over and delivered vegetables to Layton until he began working at Myers Garage as a teenager. Myers was the only place for auto repair this side of the county. Wallace had managed the place since he was nineteen.

"But you run it. Why can't you close it?"

"Walter Myers is a bit anxious over finances. I reckon I want to stay in his good graces."

They moved toward the dirt parking lot and separated. A sense of unbalance came over her. She glanced over her shoulder as he closed his auto door. *I'll miss you.* Goodness. What influence did that man have over her?

She couldn't imagine her life without him in it. Yet she wasn't sure she wanted such a predictable lifestyle.

Two days had passed since he'd pulled Clara to him at the Forder graveyard. She'd relaxed in his embrace. The memory stirred him. Wallace pulled a red rag from the pocket of his garage uniform and wiped his brow. Summer heat beat down on him. The thought of a cold Dr. Pepper teased him, but he couldn't spare the time for a walk to the store for a purchase. His workload doubled when his mechanic moved to Oklahoma. Sometime he'd need to get a cola machine in this place. Sometime he'd need to hire a new mechanic.

He had one more auto to service before calling it a day. He laughed. The auto staring at him from the other bay looked at home. Ben Williams, Clara's Papa, was a frequent customer. Wallace reckoned the auto was a means for him to get from here to there and not a point of pride.

Wallace didn't mind the frequent repairs, for Clara and her youngest brother would often walk across the street after her shift at the diner section of the Justice Restaurant to chatter while he worked on her Papa's auto. He hoped today was no exception because he had something to show her.

For almost half of his twenty-four years, he'd had feelings for Clara. The beautiful angel kiss on her cheek captivated him early on. Though not old enough to be considered a man at the time, Wallace had been mature enough to name the emotion nothing more than intrigue. Over the years as time made the age gap more respectable, his intrigue had become what it was always meant to be. He was in love with Clara. Soon he would ask to make her his wife.

He stilled. What if Clara had no intention of marrying him? Her question about his happiness two days ago at the graveyard nagged at him. Perhaps she desired more than the familiar, comfortable life he had to offer.

He shook away the despairing thought and turned his attention to her Papa's auto.

"Wallace?" His breath hitched. Clara's voice called from the garage office. He glanced at his watch. He had another half-hour of work to do.

"I'm in the bay. Come on in."

He sensed her presence and looked toward the door. Pale green fabric lay against her curves and accented the russet tendrils slipping from her knotted bun. Her appearance enticed him. He'd expected to see her in the navy diner uniform. He'd also expected to see her brother Raymond.

Wallace moved to stand before her. "You look lovely, Clara." His fingers fought to touch her, but he wrestled them with his grease rag.

"Where's Raymond?"

"He went straight home from school. I forgot you'd be here alone. I guess I should leave."

No.

"Your Papa should be dropped off soon from work, but let me open the bay door. We'll be visible and your reputation will remain honorable."

He did. She stayed. He continued to work on the auto.

"Did you work the diner today?"

"No. I ran the store register." She rubbed her palms together. "I worked on a story between customers."

Perfect. "I've something to show you." He came and sat beside her in the old metal chair next to the one he'd dubbed "hers" because she sat in it more than anyone else. He admired that she wrote values into insect stories for children.

"Clara, I read this article in Farmers Field Magazine. It might help you with your stories." He pointed to the page he had turned down. "It explains how insects hear."

She giggled. "I feel plum silly. I've never paused to think about insect ears. I reckon it's time I learned."

Wallace titled back his head and released a laugh. "Me neither." He pointed. "It says here, grasshoppers pick up sound with their legs. Mosquitos use their antennae."

He smiled at her, but was taken aback by the moisture in her eyes.

"You care about my hobby."

Oh, Clara, I care about so much more than your hobby.

"Yes, I do." He nodded as he spoke.

"Read the article to me. If you have time."

Wallace placed the magazine face down on his leg, then removed his watch from his wrist.

"What are you doing? You always wear your watch." He touched her knuckles. "I'm letting you know time doesn't matter. I give you mine. Unhurried."

She opened her mouth as to speak but didn't. A shy smile spread on her lips instead. But it was her eyes that told him her thoughts as they closed and opened. She wasn't sure she wanted all his time.

He swallowed the disappointment and read about the grasshopper.

Amidst the words she gasped and sat up in her chair. Now her eyes danced with gratitude and excitement. The change jerked him.

"Wallace, children need to know the importance of listening and not always talking. Thank you. My mind is filled with conversation and actions. A grasshopper is about to come to life on my writing tablet."

Her arms enclosed his neck. There was no passion. Only excitement. He might have gotten the same reaction from one of his sisters.

His insides ached. Clara seemed to love him and regret it.

Chapter 2
NOVEMBER 1924 | LAYTON, TEXAS

Eleven-year-old Wallace suppressed a yawn. He supposed no growing boy worthy of man's work should display his fatigue. He tugged at the buckle of his overall strap to loosen it. There was no more give. All day as he accompanied his Pa on vegetable deliveries, the strap had pressed into his shoulder. Ma teased that he was growing so much, he'd probably eat up all the business supply.

Wallace was proud to be the oldest son of Pony James, the local vegetable supplier, and even more proud to be accompanying his Pa on deliveries to learn that end of the business. Wallace was one of nine siblings, and those old enough always helped work the fields on the farm in Evans, Texas. Sitting next to his Pa all day on the wagon seat with the cool autumn breeze swirling around him was a change from bending over the black, Texas dirt. He shifted. His backside ached.

The last stop on his Pa's rounds was the Justice Store in Layton. Pa had made the people of Layton legendary with his stories around the supper table. Wallace reckoned most of them were plain folk whose attributes had been magnified by his Pa's fondness for the town and the store clientele. Well, Mr. Mason Forder, who owned most of the surrounding area and businesses in what was dubbed the Forder Empire, wasn't plain folk, but Pa said he was a good man and neighbor to the people of Layton.

The flat Texas earth gave him a peek at the town in the distance. Only a few structures stood on the ground. He could count them. If this was the center of Layton, then what did his Pa see in the town?

The motion of the cart wheels against the dirt and the pounding of the mule's feet filled the comfortable silence that had settled between he and Pa. At last, the town was displayed before him. A small depot. The store with a motel of sorts. A schoolhouse. He had to look further to see more. In the distance a sprinkling of houses sat in no order like a checkerboard abandoned mid game. Was that a church steeple in the bend in the road?

7

Before the wagon had come to a complete halt, Wallace jumped down from his seat to relieve his discomfort. He pulled his Pa's handwritten delivery list from his overall pocket and loaded his arms with a bushel of apples. Pa pulled down another and used it to prop open the store's screen door. A bell jingled to welcome them.

Wallace made his way through the doorway, sat the bushel next to the counter, then took in the scene before him. The warm air, smell of a diner, and the colors of fresh vegetables matched Pa's description.

"Pony, good to see you."

Wallace turned toward the voice behind the counter. No doubt, this was Mr. Justice of the Justice Store. Pa shook the man's hand.

"I want you to meet my oldest child, Wallace. He's learning this side of the business." Wallace took the hand extended to him. "Nice to meet you, sir."

"Well, son, the pleasure's all mine." The man winked at him. "Reckon your Pa wouldn't mind if I paid you for your labor with a cola?"

Wallace turned to his Pa, who nodded his approval and pointed. "Go help yourself. I'll finish carrying in the load and settle up. Take a look around."

He selected a root beer from the cola machine. Not once had he enjoyed a bottle to himself with no siblings begging a sip. Made the whole thing taste sweeter, and with a final gulp, he slid his palm across his mouth wiping the excess.

The doorbell jingled again. Wallace put the bottle in an empty slot in the cola crate and looked toward the entrance. A young girl with russet hair entered ahead of two women. Her high-pitched voice called out as she turned down an aisle. "Mr. Forder, where's Mary?"

Mr. Forder? Wallace turned to his left. How had he missed seeing the man in the suit? He was kneeling eye-level with the little girl and discussing birthdays. The man had a kind voice. The taller of the two women spoke with him, then led the girl to the next aisle.

Wallace moved that direction to enter the next aisle too but from the opposite side. What child could address the head of Forder empire as though he were her uncle? Perhaps he was.

Just as he rounded the corner, the tall woman brushed passed him. Wallace acknowledged her with a smile. The russet-headed little girl stood

8

before him, and he stepped closer to her. Not wishing to scare the child, he picked up a Hershey Bar and began to examine the wrapper.

"I wanted some of that chocolate. It's my favorite. But Momma says I have to get Lifesavers."

Wallace looked down at the child who had turned her face toward him. What he noticed made him suck in a breath. An angel had kissed this child. Her right cheek was graced by a light brown mark. He'd never seen such a thing until a few months ago when his baby sister was born. Like the russet-haired girl before him, the infant had a beautiful mark on her cheek. Ma said the angels were telling the world this baby had a lot of love to give and would need a lot of love in return. Ma believed she'd been placed in their family for that very reason.

His heart beat faster. The tall woman—Momma—must surely love this child a lot. Who all did the child love in return?

Wallace put the Hershey Bar back on the shelf then pointed to the rolls of candy. "Lifesavers taste good too. I like cherry the best." The girl shrugged her shoulder.

"They're my second favorite candy. Momma says I don't need chocolate 'cause I'm getting chocolate frosting on my birthday cake."

So she and Mr. Forder *had* been talking about her birthday.

"Happy Birthday."

"I'm gonna be five." A grin spread over his mouth at her confident tone. Wallace marked their age difference. Six years.

"That makes you too old to fuss about treats."

The child hoisted a hand to her hip then turned to pick up a roll of candy. "Lifesavers are more grown up candy. I like butterscotch." Wallace dare not laugh out loud. Although his sisters worked the fields, they 'd sure shown him enough prissiness that he knew not to mock it. "My baby sister has an angel kiss like yours." The child covered the mark with her empty hand. A blush crept up her face. Wallace took a step backward. Had he offended the child?

"It's ugly."

Wallace swallowed. Sad.

"I think my sister's mark is pretty special. I bet yours is too."

"Momma and my aunt says so. But not my uncle."

"I think your uncle is wrong."

The child's hand went to her side. "What's your name?'

"I'm Wallace James."

"My name is Clara Williams. I never saw you here."

"I'm helping my Pa with deliveries today. He's teaching me the job."

"My Papa doesn't do deliveries. I think his work is far away, but one day he might finish it and get to come back home. Maybe even tomorrow since it's my birthday."

Before he could reply, feet shuffled at the end of the aisle and drew his attention. He felt relief. He wouldn't have known how to reply to the girl's comment.

"Wallace." Pa.

The tall woman appeared at the other end of the aisle. She was looking at him. Aside from the russet hair and tall frame, the child looked nothing like her. Maybe he'd been mistaken and the lady wasn't Clara's Momma. She moved next to the child. Wallace moved next to his father just as Pa's attention went to the woman.

"Mrs. Williams, I believe. Good to see you."

"Hello, Mr. James. Hope you brought us some good apples."

"I most certainly did." Wallace felt Pa's pat on the shoulder.

"This here's my oldest, Wallace. He normally stays back and oversees the farm while I deliver, but today he's learning this side of the business."

The woman had a nice smile when she looked at him.

"Good to meet you, Wallace. You met my Clara?"

"Yessum. I told her happy birthday. I heard her talking about it when y'all came in."

He felt Pa's tug. "We best be going about our business, son."

"Bye Wallace." The voice came from the little girl. Wallace and his Pa waved and started out the door. Would the angel-kissed girl be in the store when he returned? He hoped so, and the feeling unsettled him.

"Pa, she was kissed by an angel, just like Sissy."

"Is that right? She must be loved a lot."

"I reckon, but her Pa works far away. She said he might be at her birthday."

Pa seemed to hesitate, opening his mouth to speak, then shutting it. At last he simply replied, "Is that so."

Wallace was curious. "Do you know him, Pa?"

"I met him once, before the girl was born."

"Oh. I reckon he does work really far away."

"I suppose. Now, tally up what's left in the wagon, and let's get home in time for supper."

"Yessir. Can I drive the wagon home?"

Pa's answer consisted of hoisting himself to the passenger side of the seat.

Wallace glanced behind him as the town of Layton faded in the distance. A russet butterfly landed next to him on the seat. He reached for it, but it flew out of sight. He thought of another sighting today and didn't try to stop his smile.

Happy Birthday to the angel-kissed child.

Chapter 3
April 1930 | Layton, Texas

Eleven-year-old Clara felt the grin spread from one ear to another. She was proud. She was excited.

She was late.

Clara stuffed the lined paper into her open school satchel then slid the straps through the buckles to close it up. After one last glance at her best friends, Maggie and Mary, she took off running down the dirt road between her school house and home.

"Bye, princesses."

She could hear her friends giggle behind her and from the corner of her eye, saw Maggie head home in the opposite direction. Mere months separated their stair-stepped ages that placed Mary between the older Clara and the younger Maggie.

Moist Texas dirt popped against the back of Clara's legs as she caught her foot in a mud puddle. No doubt, Momma would frown at her speckled skin, and remind her that young ladies avoided mud puddles. Clara rolled her eyes. Being a young lady often lacked excitement and adventure. Maggie and Mary were ladylike enough.

The role of queen, princess, and lady had rotated between them in their imaginary kingdom since the girls were four or five years old. The title of princess had stuck. But the three of them had outgrown the land of their imagination. Now images of handsome school boys, dreams of wedding gowns, and the wonder of life as women had moved in.

It's not that Clara preferred mud puddles over lace and curls. But her inside aspirations often wrestled with her outside appearance. Why avoid a mud puddle when jumping in one was exciting? She looked like a homegirl and future homemaker, but felt like a free spirit on the verge of a great adventure. Surely God had big plans waiting for her somewhere, someday. Something far more exciting than a mud puddle.

She rounded the curve in the road and slowed down to catch her breath. Her oldest brother, Jacob, was swirling a wooden sword in the air. He whispered as she passed by. "Ahoy, matey. Prepare for trouble." Their dog, Pistol Pirate, ran up and licked her leg. She rubbed his ears.

Clara spotted Momma among the crepe myrtles. Her toddler brother, Raymond, played nearby with a ball. Clara paused at the sight. Katherine Williams—pretty Momma.

Time to get the talkin' to she deserved. A twig snapped beneath her foot and drew Momma's attention. Clara noticed her lips and eyebrow relax before a stern look took over. Clara's shoulders slumped, knowing she'd worried her.

Momma's gaze moved to the hem of Clara's dress. "I see that a mud puddle slowed you down."

"No ma'am. I jumped over it, sort of. Me, Mary, and Maggie were talkin' while Mary waited for her brother to come get her. The teacher came out and shooed us away."

"You're the oldest child, but make me fret more than your little brothers."

At the mention of the oldest, an image of Sammy came to Clara' mind. He was the half-brother she'd never known. When she'd learned of Sammy, her four-year-old heart had formed a bond with the image of his existence. They shared a Papa, though their lives never touched. His ended before hers began. He'd known the Papa she'd never met at the time of discovering Sammy's grave.

"I should have left right when the bell rang. I'm sorry, Momma." Katherine smiled. "I wouldn't trade your spunk and spirit. You just need to control it sometimes."

"Yessum."

"I spared your Papa the worry, since he's busy building the dining room."

Clara hugged Momma. "Why do we need a dining room? We got a kitchen?" Little Raymond toddled over. Clara bent and kissed his sweaty head then tossed back the ball he handed to her. Momma grinned. "A dining room will hold a big table for lots of people. An eating adventure."

Clara gasped. She slid the satchel from her shoulder and presented lined paper filled with her best penmanship. "Momma, it's my adventure story from school. I got a perfect score." She felt her mouth spread into a large smile.

Momma took the paper. "Flutterby's Adventure." Clara giggled. "I wrote about a butterfly since I am one." Momma laughed. "Yes, you're Papa's Little Butterfly." Warm fingers clasped her hand and led Clara to a tree. The two of them sat and nestled in. Little Raymond crawled into Clara's lap and piled dirt on her school dress while Momma read aloud, but Clara didn't care. Her attention was focused on Momma's voice and expressions.

The story ended. Momma's eyes locked with hers. "Your story is so good." Raymond reached for the paper, but Momma handed it back. "Since Jacob is good at making things with wood, I'm gonna ask him to make a frame we can slide these pages into. I'll hang it in the house."

Clara felt pride surge through her. "And, since Aunt Lena drew butterflies in my butterfly book, maybe she could draw Flutterby and"

"And we could hang that too." Momma pulled Clara in for hug, when Raymond, who'd chased after a bird pointed. "Look" Clara followed his finger and discovered a large ant bed. She and Momma made their way toward it, observing a trail of ants traveling to and from the pile of dirt. "Ants are hard workers. I reckon they never give up until the job is done." Momma picked up Raymond as she spoke, then moved away from the bed.

"Clara, you should write more stories. God gave you a gift for that."

"I want to, but I don't know what to write about."

Momma paused and looked her in the eye. "It'll come to ya. Be like the ants and don't give up."

Leaving them behind, Clara moseyed toward the back door. Male voices and the sounds of hammers and saws lingered in the air. Just as she rounded the corner of the house, Wallace James walked out of the family's shed, holding a screwdriver. They paused.

Wallace was tall. Wallace was handsome. Wallace was a teenager. The princesses had just giggled over Wallace in the school yard.

Clara rued her muddy hem. Surely Wallace wouldn't cast his large eyes there.

"Why are you here?" Her hand went to her hip. Wallace lived miles away in Evan on his family's vegetable farm, but worked in Layton most Saturdays. Some Friday afternoons and Saturdays. Papa and the preacher went rabbit hunting with he and his Pa. A couple of years ago, the James family started driving into Layton for Sunday services. So overall, Wallace was no stranger. In fact, she'd always reckoned him like a big brother she didn't see much.

He laughed. "Pa and me are in town, so we're helping your Papa build the dining room."

"Oh. I thought Uncle Henry was helping. '

"Him too."

"I heard Momma say Papa needed lots of help 'cause he wasn't a natural. Somethin' like that."

Wallace tossed his head back and laughed before speaking again.

"Me and Pa brought my stuff from home. I'm moving to the spare room at Myers Garage tonight."

Clara felt her eyes widen. "You'll live there by yourself?" *What an adventure.*

"Yep. I'm seventeen, and old enough to be on my own. I'll work every day now. Not just the weekends."

Clara wanted to say something intelligent or at least not ignorant, but her tongue tied, and nothing came out. A strange sensation moved over her and her face heated. *Giggles. Blush. Goosebumps. Oh goodness, I've got a fancy for Wallace.* The realization embarrassed her. And bothered her. After all, it's Wallace. Big brother. Papa's hunting partner. Local mechanic. Practically old and boring.

He pointed to the papers in her hands. "What's that." She shook away her thoughts. "A story I wrote at school."

He stuffed the screwdriver into his pocket and reached for the pages. "Can I read it?"

"Doesn't Papa need your help?"

He smiled. "I'm a fast reader."

Her stomach knotted. She held out the papers for him to grasp. "Don't laugh."

He didn't.

In fact he went slack-jawed.

"Clara, this is a mighty good story. You should write more."

"You really think so?"

"I do."

The simple reply settled in like a hunch.

He handed her the papers and walked away with a thanks.

She stood there, unsettled.

Chapter 4

Noon. Clara sighed. She'd worked on this story for more than two hours, yet all she had to show for it were hints of a story rubbed out on paper made thin by an eraser. Words had been needy and obstinate today of all days. In a rare collision of events, she found herself alone in the house, disappointed that the occasion produced nothing. She twirled a lock of her russet hair around a finger. She'd tried to force her creativity. Even her childhood butterfly art book, that served as inspiration, had failed her, looking worn and overused in the lamplight. She gathered her items to put them away for another day. Well, another hour snatched here and there between life.

Just last week she'd been jubilant over the month's events of turning twelve, celebrating Thanksgiving, and making ribbons for the Christmas tree that would soon adorn the front room. She supposed contentment didn't necessarily promise a good story line. Who knew pudgy little bumblebees could be so difficult to write about? The first two insect stories she wrote had flown from her mind faster than her hand could put the words to paper. Maybe writing insect stories that taught children important lessons wasn't her niche.

It was and she knew it. Doubt settled in. Who cared about her dumb stories anyway? A parade of folks passed through her mind. Family cared. She had to smile.

Clara glanced around the room that Momma had recently spruced up, as she called it. The front room boasted new wallpaper with flowers on it. The rockers, a staple in the room since the days when Momma didn't even know Papa existed, had new cushion covers. The windows and breeze puffed out new curtains. And over the mantle, hung her Flutterby story and drawing. It kept watch on the only picture of Sammy her family possessed, a rabbit's foot resting in a ceramic bowl, and various what-nots on the mantle. Unto themselves, they told the story of her and her kin.

And right next to her brothers' bedroom door was the perfect place for a telephone. Momma resisted getting such a contraption, stating everyone she loved and needed to talk to were within walking distance. Clara chuckled. She certainly didn't get her adventurous spirit from Momma.

Thunder shouted the promise of a storm. Clara enjoyed a light mist, but had always found storms unsettling.

Commotion on the front steps startled her. She dropped her items into the rocker. Papa and the boys were at Myers Garage waiting a repair, her brothers no doubt talking Wallace's ear off and trying to handle every tool and piece of equipment they could. Momma was working the books at the Justice Store. Who could be at the door?

"Katherine!" Clara jumped at the sound of Uncle Henry's voice. She yanked open the door. "Momma's at the store." Henry, usually kempt, had hair pointing in every direction. His eyes bulged. His clothes were wrinkled.

"Get over to the house. Lena's in labor. It's too early. She's almost writhing in pain. My little boy is crying, thinking his mother is dying. He don't understand about babies being born."

"Go get the midwife, Celeste."

"I am." His breaths came quickly. "Lena needs her sister though."

Clara grabbed his shoulders. "Uncle Henry, go get in your auto, stop at the store, bring Momma here, then head out to get Celeste." She closed the door behind her. "I'll go take care of your family."

Clara walked the short path between their houses, frightened over what she'd discover. The air was heavy with moisture. Clara remembered when Uncle Henry bought his home from the Sears Catalog years before. A well-worn path between the two houses bore witness to the frequent comings and goings of the household members. The families were as knit as two hands with fingers intertwined. Indeed, Henry and Lena's family were her only blood relatives outside of her parents and brothers.

But today only fear seemed to saturate the air on the path as screams came from within the house. Maybe she was too young at the time to remember, but Clara couldn't recall Momma's screams sounding like this when her brothers were born. She pushed open the front door to discover her little cousin, Robert, huddled next to a chair. "Here, here, little buddy, I know you're scared. You sit right here in this chair, and I'll come rock you after I check on Mommy."

Her twelve years rolled back to four, and she trembled as she nudged the bedroom door, then closed it gently. The room was thick with darkness, heat, and dread. Lena writhed in the bed, moaning. Was she conscious?

"Aunt Lena?"

Whimpers answered. "My baby is dying." Clara choked back her own whimper. "Maybe the baby is just upside down." She didn't know what that meant, but Momma had said it one day about the woman who sold poinsettias outside the store at Christmas time. Her baby turned out fine and would probably be running around the lot this year when it was time to sell the plants.

"I don't know." Lena let out a groan then sprang up and doubled over pressed by obvious pain. She emitted a scream. Clara grabbed a wash rag from the bedside table. When Lena relaxed and lay back down, she wiped her brow. Lena pushed her hand away. "Where's Henry? Henry!" Clara stroked her arm. "Shh. Shh. He's gone to get Momma at the store and Celeste." Lena began to outright cry. "My baby. Somethins' wrong with my baby."

Clara held her aunt's hand, aware that a little child in the next room was scared and alone. She whispered prayers to God that this baby and Lena would survive whatever was happening. Aunt Lena had been around enough births, Clara suspected, that she could sense when something was terribly wrong.

"Lena." Momma's voice. At the sound of it, Clara couldn't suppress her tears any longer and let them roll freely down her cheeks and neck. She stood, and after a squeeze of Momma's hand, slipped from the room. As she closed the door, Lena's wails increased. "Oh, Katherine, I think my baby is dead."

Clara made her way to the front room while holding her sobs inside for the sake of cousin Robert. She grabbed him up and headed out. No need for him to hear his mother wailing. But as they moved through the front door, his whimpers became their own wails. He squirmed and reached back for his Mommy. Clara held him tight against her so she wouldn't drop him. Just as she entered the path between the houses, an auto skid into the drive, and Henry shot out from the passenger side. Clara squinted. Papa was driving.

Little Robert called out for his own Papa. Clara made her way back to where Uncle Henry had stilled at the porch steps. He pulled his son to him and immediately his neck was gripped by the child's small arms. "Little Buddy, Papa loves you. For a bit, I'm gonna take care of Mommy, and Clara is gonna take care of you." He kissed the boy's cheek and edged him back to her.

Papa called from the auto. "I'm going to get Celeste." As he did, Wallace and her brothers were exiting the backseat. They headed her way and the group of them walked the path. Wallace's deep voice broke the silence. "Your Papa thought I could help with the youngins'. He's afraid it might be awhile. And he didn't want you alone." Clara nodded her agreement, and they moved on in silence. She was relieved to have someone with her, and deep inside at a time when selfish thoughts shouldn't surface, she was pleased the someone was Wallace.

Her girlhood crush hadn't faded. And unfortunately, neither had her nervous affliction. The first hiccup escaped with no warning. She felt her face blush, but the slight giggle from little Robert and the smile from the young man next to her eased the mortification.

Wallace entertained the boys in the front room of Clara's family home while she made jelly sandwiches. Her hiccups echoing in the silent kitchen. She held her breath and counted to ten, knowing full well the remedy against the ailment was useless. She managed to fit a command to come eat between two spasms.

Clara urged Robert to eat by playing choo choo tunnel with his food while Wallace made sure Raymond didn't spill his milk.

"Are you alright?" The sound was that of the big brother figure she'd known him to be. "I'm s-c-a-r-e-d." She spelled the word with no interruptions. Good. Her hiccups had ceased. Wallace nodded his understanding.

Lightening lit up the room. The storm had arrived. Robert and Raymond yelped. She glanced at the man across from her. "Don't worry, fellas, I'll keep you safe." His words were for the boys, but the assurance was for her. His eye contact made that clear.

According to Henry, Wallace relayed, Momma had taken off running from the store, but Carl Justice had grabbed her and insisted he drive her the mile to Lena's.

Clara smiled at the thought of Carl Justice, and his wife, Louise. They managed the store, but more and more, their health prevented them from being there. Uncle Henry, who ran the small motel and diner connected to the business, had eased into managing the store as well. The Justice's were grandparent figures to Clara and her brothers, and even little Robert.

———◆———

There are moments when time stands still and no day is distinct from the other. For Clara, this sensation began before the evening set in. A little girl was stillborn. Friends came and went. Those like family lingered. A private burial. An emptiness. A silence. Somehow time had passed, but no one noticed.

And then, a darkness set in, not only in the country as it struggled financially, but also in Clara's own small world.

Uncle Henry as she'd known him, was gone. His humor became sarcasm. His joy gave way to hopelessness. His energy cowered to deep sleep. Never was he left alone. Never did Aunt Lena subject him to horrid treatments in a hospital. And for weeks following the loss of a baby girl, Aunt Lena was the only light to draw Henry from his despair—moments at a time. When she did, the affection between husband and wife, and father and little son gave hope for recovery. Clara witnessed these scenes time after time.

And on no particular morning after summer had set in, Uncle Henry walked into the kitchen while Clara and her family ate. Little Robert clasped one hand while Aunt Lena clasped the other. "Before I head to work today…"

Clara was certain her smile touched her earlobes. Momma gasped. Papa stood. Work. Today.

"…we've got an announcement." Henry winked, and suddenly Clara knew that once again minutes created hours, the day's marked themselves with names, and the world caught up. The darkness had been covered with light.

And before the butterflies danced their migration in the Fall, Aunt Lena's middle swelled as it carried the future beneath her heart.

Chapter 5

February 1933 | Layton, Texas

The girl in his arms was pretty. Wallace would even call her sweet. And for the life of him, he couldn't reason why none of that mattered. Her faith, her face, her figure, her friendliness all failed to attract him.

Perhaps if she wrote children's stories or had russet curls or sassed him when he perturbed her, he might feel differently.

None of that described Patricia Ann.

He was certainly of the marrying age and certainly tired of living in the back room of Myers Garage. But he certainly didn't want to attach himself to someone he didn't care for. He'd prefer loneliness over regret.

He shouldn't have dabbled with Patricia Ann's emotions by spending time with her. She was the third young woman he'd given any amount of attention to since he was sixteen, and the third one that failed to spark a flicker of future and family.

The fiddlers changed the tune to a more upbeat rhythm, and Wallace guided Patricia Ann into a dance that left more distance between them. She smiled—and he thought it a lovely sight. Maybe he needed more time to take a likin' to her. Maybe he should court her.

His day had been awful. Economic reality had set in. For him to maintain a job, he'd have to give up some of his pay to the owner. The last thing he wanted was to be jobless like so many others in the nation. He'd hoped the church dance and pantry drive would free his mind, but that hope was lost the moment Clara and the Williams family walked through the doors of the small community center outside of town.

On second thought, maybe he shouldn't court Patricia Ann. Maybe he'd wait until Clara was a respectable age. He chuckled. He'd be twenty-four. He'd been struck by her spunk and her angel kiss when he first laid eyes on her at the Justice Store almost nine years ago.

Wallace, get your thoughts in line.

"Did you hear me?" The sound of agitation in Patricia Ann's voice caught his ear. No, he hadn't heard a thing she'd said since the music changed.

22

"I'm sorry." He smiled. "I guess I didn't."

"I said, thank you for bringing me here. I'm enjoying myself. I like your company."

Wallace stammered through the only truthful response he had. "I appreciate your comin' with me."

The look of disappointment on her face stung. *I'm a worthless scoundrel.* He mustered words that he could speak with sincerity. "You're a lovely lady, Patricia Ann. I believe no young woman in here outshines you."

He'd not lied, for Clara was a young teenager, and a recent one at that.

The song ended and the emcee announced for everyone to clear the dance floor. Wallace led his date to a table and joined Pastor and Amy Carlson. Their daughter Maggie sat beside her mother. Wallace noticed her face turn beet red when their eyes caught one another. Had he and Patricia Ann interrupted a private conversation?

The sound of young boys playing tag outside wafted through the open door of the building. Patricia Ann's voice mingled with theirs. "Hello, everyone." His date smiled and continued speaking. "Maggie, you look so pretty in pink. Are you playing the piano for us tonight?" Maggie nodded. Wallace shifted in his seat remembering that Patricia Ann oversaw socials for the girls at church. She knew Maggie fairly well. And Clara.

What little lingering thought of courting the woman dissipated. No way could he marry her and risk having Clara socializing with and probably confiding in his would-be wife. Nope. Patricia Ann was meant for someone else. He was most likely meant to be a bachelor, if not for a lifetime, then for a few more respectable years that would feel like a lifetime.

Pastor Carlson slid back his seat. "Well, I'm up next." He patted his daughter. "You're number three on the entertainment schedule." Wendell Carlson made his way toward the stage as the emcee whistled to quiet everyone. After kind words of thanks for the contributions and a prayer for the needy sitting right here among them, Pastor Carlson introduced the first performer in local entertainment. Wallace felt his heart speed up.

"So, with no further introduction needed, let's welcome our home town storyteller, Clara Williams, who will share one of her recent works with us." Wallace joined in the applause and shifted his chair for a more straight on view, careful not to turn his back to Patricia Ann. And for the next fifteen minutes, Clara entertained a room filled with folks who knew her, cared for her, and flat out admired her talent. At least, Wallace assumed that others felt the same way he did about her. Truth be told, he was quite proud of Clara, like a big brother would be, and with the help of the good Lord's guidance, he'd leave it at that for now.

Half an hour later Wallace couldn't help but notice the wind picking up outside. Another Texas thunderstorm could be coming out of nowhere. With each hand full of cookies, he made his way to the back of the room. The bingo game was the next order of business for the evening. He'd never enjoyed the game, but did enjoy watching folks react when they hit bingo. He stood himself in a corner to observe. Patricia Ann sat next to Lena and Henry at a bingo table.

"Are you being a fuddy-duddy Wallace?" Good grief. Had he blushed? Clara Williams stood in front of him, hands on her hips, flanked by Mary and Maggie. He shoved a small peanut butter cookie into his mouth and spoke before swallowing. "Nope. Just enjoying my cookies." Mary spoke up. "Maggie made those." Wallace swallowed at the same time he acknowledged the baker. "Good cookies, Maggie." She giggled. "Thank you. I can make you some anytime." Wallace shifted his position. No thanks. He nodded. "How kind." Meanwhile, Clara had turned toward the tables where the bingo cards lay, and took a step away.

No.

"Good story, Clara." She swiveled and faced him. "Thank you. It's the one I finished at the garage while Raymond and me was waitin' on Papa to come back with the colas from the store. You know, when the auto had a bad brake," she exaggerated the auto's condition, "and Papa dragged me and Raymond with him to get it fixed." She grinned.

"I remember. While your Momma was settin' up your surprise birthday party."

"Yep." She grabbed a hand of both girls. "Let's git. Bingo's starting."

Wallace remembered his manners, and called out as they left. "And beautiful song on the piano, Maggie." She hollered back a thanks, but it was Clara's words that sunk in. He wasn't meant to hear them.

"He's handsome, but he's like my big brother."

Bingo.

Having gobbled the rest of the cookies, Wallace made his way to other end of the building. Local amateur veterinarian, Gabriel, and his wife stood near the open side door, apparently keeping an eye on the creatures outside. He'd brought baby goats for the youngins to pet. He wondered if the couple realized the animals' aroma made its way inside the large room. Apparently not. "Evening Gabriel…" He was unable to finish his greeting before a large gust of air blew in, scattering loose paper napkins from the tables here and there. Wallace jerked to attention. And loose writing tablet papers. Clara's story.

Wallace chased after the pieces floating through the air. He could hear Gabriel behind him doing the same thing. Wallace made his way out the side door to retrieve whatever he could find. Two pieces of paper lay against the outside of the building, as though they were catching their breath before taking off again. He reached for them both, noting that one was the title page. In haste without hesitation, he folded that page and shoved it in his pants pocket. Clara could write another title page, and he'd have a small piece of her to hold on to.

Shameful, he reckoned, but not enough to stop him.

"Find any?" Gabriel's voice pushed through his cleft pallet. Wallace nodded. He'd not lie. "Yep." He handed the piece of paper to Gabriel's wife who seemed to be putting them back in order. "I'll take these to Clara," she said to her husband.

"Bingo!" Clara's voice. She'd won. The reaction stopped Gabriel's wife in her tracks. Wallace clapped and whistled with the others as Clara moved to the prize table and selected a metal WWI toy airplane. For her brothers no doubt. Wallace smiled. Prizes in good condition had been donated by families who could part with items. Wallace watched as Mary leaned toward Clara and whispered something after she sat back down. The interaction evoked a hug between them. Wallace figured the toy plane had belonged to Mary's older brother. He didn't know any other family in their community who could have made such a purchase.

25

Wallace meandered outside through the front doors and leaned against his auto. A hint of guilt pinched him. Snatching the title page had been childish and deceptive. "Lord, I just took something that's not mine, but here I am praying. I can't push this feeling about Clara out of my heart. If it ain't right, I need you to push it out. I won't argue with you if you'll just make it go away." His words were between him and God.

A petite hand touched his forearm. "Patricia Ann." He hadn't heard her approach. The evening light made her features glow, but he stood there unmoved by her presence. "Bingo over?" She nodded. He smiled. "Did you win anything?" She nodded differently. "Do you want some more punch?" She raised her eyebrows. "Yes, and so you won't have to ask, I'd like a piece of sweet potato pie too." He was leading her inside when Raymond bound into his legs. "Sorry, Wallace."

"Nice plane."

"That man named Garrett used to play with it. Now it's mine and Jacob's." He took off making a wind sound and swooshing the toy plane up and down in the air. Patricia Ann giggled. "He's so cute." Wallace had to agree.

Just as they reached the punch table, Clara appeared on the opposite side of it. "I been looking for you. Thanks, Wallace, for helping Gabriel get my pages." She hugged the paper to her. "All here. Well, 'cept the title page." He cleared his throat to confess, but her words spared him the humiliation. "That's nothing to worry about."

Exactly. Taking the title page was nothing to worry about.

"You're welcome, Clara." She threw out a good-bye to them both, leaving Wallace to explain things to Patricia Ann.

"You're a good man, Wallace James."

Then he best act like one. "Excuse me, Patricia Ann." He moved in quick steps to catch Clara and somehow explain how he had the paper, but saw her slip out the door with Ben and Katherine.

On second thought, he would toss the paper outside when he went to his auto.

He shouldn't have it in his possession.

Chapter 6

Enjoy the waitin'. Wallace shifted his crouched position in the tall grass and shook his head back and forth, then wiped August sweat from his brow. Pa's mantra for rabbit hunting nagged at him today. Pa engrained in him the importance of patience when it came to hunting. As Wallace matured, he'd come to realize that Pa's advice had as much to do with life as it did with the hunt. But not today. Wallace had determined that in at least one aspect of life, he had grown weary of enjoying the wait.

And the man crouched next to him could help bring his wait to an end. After all, Clara would soon turn eighteen. And at twenty-four, he waited long enough.

Ben Williams roused from his position in the grass and stood next to Wallace, then looked left and motioned to Pa who was crouched yards away. Wallace rose. Ben pointed to Wallace's gun. He was to take the lead as they moved deeper into the open field.

Wallace's voice hadn't begun to change when Clara's Papa and the local pastor had become hunting partners with he and Pa. Wallace missed Pastor Carlson today who was too ill for hunting. He'd likely miss many hunts before he recovered from a burst appendix.

Wallace acknowledged Ben's motion with a nod and the three of them set out in a horizontal line. The uneven rhythm of Ben's limp a familiar sound to him.

One, two, three, four, five—Wallace reached ten paces and held up his hand to stop the others. Pa had taught him to take ten paces, stop, count to thirty real slow, and look around. The silence scared the rabbits and sent them fleeing to safety. Wallace looked around. No rabbits in sight. He paced again. When five rounds of pacing yielded nothing, he held up his index finger. He'd lead one more round, then pass the lead to his Pa. He counted for his final time and just as he stood still, he spotted a white tail scampering through the grass. He raised his gun and aimed. Pa's gun sounded to his left. Ben's went off to his right. His white tale had been among friends.

The three men knelt in a clearing to clean their prey. Wallace dropped his knife then wiped his hands on his overalls. This setting relaxed him, and he wanted to wait no longer. He glanced at his Pa before speaking and was glad the man would hear his conversation.

"Ben," he looked the man in the eyes. "I'd like your permission to propose to Clara."

No need to hem haw around.

He heard Pa clear his throat. Ben continued to dress his rabbit.

"I've been waiting for your question."

"I've been respectful of Clara's age."

Clara's father stilled his knife and made eye contact.

"I reckoned that and 'preciate it. Do you love her?"

"Yes." *She consumes me.*

"I reckoned that too. She's fond of you, no doubt, but does she love you? Fondness is a weak foundation for a marriage. "

"That's what I aim to find out. I'll court her right and proper if I need to."

"You have my blessing. You better cherish Clara. She's my Little Butterfly."

Wallace smiled. He fancied the nickname between father and daughter

"I already do."

Wallace had another question for Ben but left it unspoken because the answer wouldn't sway his intended pursuit.

Would Ben Williams remain a friend once he became a father-in-law?

———————◆◆◆◆———————

Clara doted over Mary Forder and Maggie Carlson. They formed a trio of lifetime friends sitting at the Carlson's kitchen table creating a pecan pie. The kitchen was heavy with heat despite the open window.

"Maggie, you're such a good piano player. Maybe you should try out for the Dallas Symphony."

Clara giggled at Mary's suggestion. Her friend embraced the magnitude of life and its possibilities.

"I'm not that good. Besides I want to be a teacher."

"You could marry a preacher and be a teacher." Mary laughed.

"I declare. I'm never marrying a preacher. And I want to teach right here in Layton."

Clara considered the preacher's daughter who was predictable and preferred life to be that way. "Who would you want to marry around here?" Clara wrapped her question in genuine curiosity, but received a shrug for an answer as Maggie blushed.

"I'll go wherever my husband takes me. As soon as I meet him." Mary teased. "But I do love our town."

"That's because it sits in the middle of your father's empire."

Clara gasped. She'd never known Maggie to be careless with words. Perhaps predictable no longer described the preacher's daughter. "Maggie, be respectful. And kind. Mr. Forder has been gone less than a year." Clara was taken aback by demand she issued her friend.

"Clara's right. I'm sorry Mary. Your father was a good, God-fearin' man who helped this community. I know you miss him."

"Terribly." Mary sniffled, then rested her hand on Clara's arm. "You're bound to be a famous author."

"I'm a writer. And glad family and friends read my stories without yawning." She covered her mouth and sighed.

"A writer who wants to marry one particular tall, handsome friend." Mary clicked her tongue.

"I'm not sure what I want. I love my home and my people, but I'm restless."

Maggie dropped the rolling pen. "But what about Wallace? Don't you want to marry him and live here. *Like me?*"

Clara's stomach stirred. Like me?

"I don't know, Maggie."

"I would know. All our years growing around him, we've seen what a good person he is. Clara Williams, you'd be lucky to have Wallace as a husband."

"And he'd be lucky to have her." Mary chided.

Clara's skin tingled when Maggie looked away before making eye contact. "Yes, he would be lucky."

A mist covered her friend's eyes.

———•◆•———

Clara yawned. The morning baking at Maggie's had caught up to her. She dropped the last clothespin into her apron, then hoisted the laundry basket to her hip. Late August was hot so the clothes took no time to dry on the line. She reckoned she'd save the ironing until the evening when the air inside the house was cooler. She turned toward the back porch and paused.

Clara's family lived humbly. She knew no dwelling other than where she presently lived—one that five generations had called home. Many times over the years, Papa had offered Momma a new house, always receiving the same answer of no, but thank you.

Indeed, Papa had made sure his family had the necessities and even many luxuries that he could afford. Except the telephone that Momma refused. The house had been renovated, updated, and expanded throughout Clara's lifetime. Papa teased Momma that the only thing original left in the house was her. She'd laugh and kiss his cheek, then remind him that the wall clock was original too.

Clara swallowed a lump in her throat. Her life wouldn't change much if Wallace proposed and she married him. After all, it was assumed among her friends that he would. The man had courted few women, and Clara was almost an official adult herself. He'd always shown decorum, despite the attraction between them. The day of Mason Forder's funeral was the first time the flicker had been spoken aloud between them.

Clara felt torn inside. She was glad he'd not married anyone, but if she married him, life would carry on much like Momma and Papa and her dear Aunt Lena and Uncle Henry. Happy families leading normal lives. Good lives considering what the country was going through.

The life Maggie wished for.

"Dear God, why can't I be content?" The tug wearied her. She felt no better than a child pitching a fit over candy.

"Clara."

Aunt Lena appeared from the clearing nestled among the crepe myrtles separating their homes. Clara strolled to the house with her. Lena opened the door.

"You're frowning. Is something wrong?" They headed into the kitchen and Clara set down the basket. "How can everything be wrong when nothing is wrong?" Lena crinkled her eyes. "Because something is bothering you." Clara huffed. "I'm bored, Aunt Lena. I want more than I see in front of me. Am I awful?" Lena shook her head no. "How you act if you don't get more is what matters." She chuckled. "Or if you do, I reckon."

Aunt Lena had been her partner in imaginary adventures all her life. Unlike Momma, Lena had never been a homebody in spirt, nor had Papa. Clara possessed that same spirit, releasing it in her stories. Lately pencil and paper had lost their power to appease the longing.

"Clara, life shows itself moments at a time. What you see now may not be what you see tomorrow." Lena took hold of her hands and squeezed. "Be glad you can't see too far ahead, 'cause as you're looking you might see things you wished you didn't."

"I ask God to make me content."

"I reckon a grateful heart is a content heart."

Clara lowered her head. Had her prayers voiced appreciation as much frustration?

Lena released her. "I'm done preachin' at you. I came to borrow back my vanilla while your Momma is working the books at the store." Clara chuckled. Lena pulled a bottle of vanilla from the cabinet, winked, and walked back out the door. Lena and Henry had their fair share of trials, especially when her uncle's moods shifted to dark, yet they were some of the happiest folk in her life. Perhaps Aunt Lena truly knew the secret to contentment was gratefulness.

Clara's stomach growled. She snatched two small yellow apples from the bowl on the table and headed to the front porch. These would hold off her hunger for now. If Papa didn't get home soon with a rabbit and start cooking his secret stew recipe, she'd need to start some other sort of supper. Clara sat on the porch steps to wait on him. Laughter and chatter filled the warm air as her brothers and cousins played tag in the yard.

At last, the pop of gravel signaled the arrival of Wallace's auto. She tossed an empty core toward the side yard. Papa emerged with a cloth bag slung over his shoulder. "Stew's gonna be mighty good tonight. We all three got a big 'ol rabbit."

Clara rose, just as her oldest brother, twelve-year-old brother Jacob, came around the corner yelling time out to those chasing him. He peeked into the bag. "Double the cornbread, Clara." He took off as abruptly as he'd stopped without yelling time in. Would be captors hastened across the yard.

Papa grinned. "I'm cleaning up then starting on the stew. Wallace is sharing his rabbit and eatin' with us." The man himself positioned himself on the step. She offered him an apple then sat back down next to him. His presence embraced her. Clara couldn't help but notice how handsome he was. Had it been this morning when she'd doubted she wanted to marry him? She smothered that discomfort with words.

"So, this wasn't a good hunt?"

Wallace blew out a breath and touched one of her curls. "Best one ever."

"But you only got one."

"I got what I wanted." He smiled. "What did you do today?"

"Me and Mary went and made pies at Maggie's. She was watching over Pastor."

"How's her pa doing?" He crunched on the apple.

"He was asleep all morning."

Clara gazed at him. "Maggie is acting weird these last few weeks. It's like she's mad at me and Mary."

"Maybe she's worried about her pa."

"Maybe. But it's like I don't know her now."

"Clara, if you want to know people, look at their eyes. Their stories are shadowed behind them."

She thought of the looks between Momma and Papa. Did Wallace know how much she desired such a look of intense love?

While the Rain Whispered

She picked an Indian Paintbrush growing near the steps. As her youngest brother ran past them, Wallace grabbed him by the waist and pulled him against his leg. Raymond laughed and fought being tickled. "What do you see in these eyes, Clara?" She laughed and bent toward Raymond. "Mischief and humor." She kissed him on the cheek. "Eww." Raymond shrieked, and Wallace released him.

"What do you see in my eyes, Wallace?" He tilted her chin up and held it with his finger. "Goodness. And Longing. Longing for something you haven't experienced or haven't gotten." She blinked to hide the truth. He let her chin drop. "And what do you see in mine?" His grin was mischievous.

Clara swallowed. She knew love and longing were reflected there, yet she wouldn't dare admit that truth. "Honesty. And an evil pleasure in killing little bunny rabbits." He laughed, but not until a hint of disappointment shown in his eyes.

Clara turned from the look. It was then a realization struck her. Whenever Maggie talked of Wallace, her eyes twinkled. She jerked her head back to the man.

"Maggie is sweet on you, Wallace. I just figured that out." He smirked. "Did she say that?" Clara stood and looked down at him. "She didn't have to. It's in her eyes."

Her own filled with tears, and again, she blinked to hide the truth. Jealousy had caught Clara Williams and tagged her on the shoulder.

Chapter 7

At last August heat had given way to cooler September breezes. Clara arched her head against the tree trunk where she rested and let the gentle wind dance around her face. A glance in the distance hinted at rain. She gathered her writing tablet, pencils, and butterfly book. She'd not written a word this afternoon. Instead her mind drifted in and out of prayer, fighting against frustration.

Was the town of Layton all God intended for her? Life here was a dandelion while she preferred a rose garden. Why had the Creator placed such longings in her, yet kept them unfulfilled? Since her talk with Lena, she'd been thanking Him best she knew how, but the tugging still lingered.

Between conversations with God this afternoon, she'd drawn two butterflies on the back page in her book and named them Wallace and Clara. Wavering demanded an aspirin. She made her way into the bathroom and swallowed relief before changing into her diner uniform. Her shift was short today. Good thing, since Momma had plans for a special dinner tonight.

Dinner. She snickered at the word. Hers was a supper kind of family, except for the hankerings Momma had every now and then. And when the hankerings were in charge, the lot of them came to the dining room table in their Sunday best.

Clara adjusted the waist of her uniform and huffed. She felt lopsided in the crooked thing, and downright gangly. A glance at her dresser mirror reminded her that at least the navy color complimented her hair. She grabbed her coat. The brown wool bragged of wear and carried the scent of her soap with a hint of yesterday's special at the diner. She'd need to hang it in the store's office on the hook behind Momma's desk instead of the diner closet.

"Bye, Momma. "A cherished voice sounded from the kitchen. "Try not to be late."

"I'll skedaddle as soon as I can." She enjoyed the word rolling off her tongue.

Despite the cold, she'd walk the mile to work. Papa drove their auto every day to his office, and she knew Uncle Henry had already driven in to work for the day. She sighed. Mason Forder had been both men's boss. He'd trusted Papa with Forder Cotton and Lumber across his vast business empire and Uncle Henry with Justice Motel, General Store, and Restaurant with its attached diner. He'd managed to keep both her Papa and uncle employed despite the Depression. Whether walking or driving to work, Clara and her clan were grateful God provided through the Forders—which made her restlessness for something more seem selfish and trivial.

Clara paced her steps to balance cold toes and the threat of a blister on her heel. Her breath hovered near her face, but didn't block Clara's view of the weeping willow cove. In the summer, slender leaves drew water from the nearby stream. Clara favored the spot for writing.

The blast of an auto horn made her trip. She rolled her eyes and laughed as Maggie's mother slowed to a stop on the opposite side of the road and rolled down her window.

"Clara Williams, it's too cold to be walking to work. Get in here now. Besides, it's fixin' to rain."

They'd just passed the store, no need for them backtrack.

Clara looked through the open window and saw Maggie agreeing by motioning her inside. Though she was halfway to the diner, the ride would probably thwart the blister. "Aw right. Thanks." She made her way to Maggie's side where an open door welcomed her.

"Just sit in my lap." Did Maggie think them still five years old? Clara bit back the retort and plopped herself onto Maggie's coat. She could feel Maggie's breath. "Hold on." Clara fell against the closed door. Mrs. Carlson's warning was too late. She turned the car in the middle of the road. The ride was plum crazy. Clara imagined the pastor's wife in goggles and a leather cap and laughed.

When the auto pulled in front of the store, Clara looked across the road to Myer's Garage. Wallace's auto, a usual fixture, wasn't parked outside. "He's not there." Clara startled at Maggie's voice. "Oh."

No matter, she'd see him soon enough. "We just left him in Greenville."

Clara reached for the door handle, wondering why any of them had been in nearby Greenville.

"Why were y'all with him?" Jealousy nagged her.

"We had coffee at the drugstore."

Clara slid from her friend's lap, but focused on her face.

"After we ran into him there." Mrs. Carlson added.

Oh. Maggie's half-truths formed a new headache.

"He was in Greenville buying some auto parts. We were buying fabric." Clara appreciated the stern look Mrs. Carlson aimed at Maggie as she explained. "We happened to stop for coffee at the same time."

"Oh." She stood upright. "Speaking of coffee, I got to get inside. Thanks for the ride."

Just as she closed the door, Clara grinned. Had any of them realized she'd be walking back home in the cool weather? The grin slumped and formed a frown. Had her friend taken pleasure in misleading her?

"Howdy, Uncle Henry." Clara stopped to go around the store counter and offer a hug. "What's that frown on your face, Clara girl?" She shrugged. "Nothing. Just girl stuff." Henry patted her shoulder. "I'm heading out early and can drive you home." He tweaked her nose. "I got dinner plans tonight." Clara welcomed his humor. "Why, so do I."

Clara rubbed the crick in her neck. This had been a busy work day. She checked the schedule on the wall and deciphered the scribbles. Sure enough tomorrow was her Saturday off. Uncle Henry joked that he took care to give his favorite niece a Saturday to herself ever once in a while. Of course, she was his only niece, but that didn't' taint his kindness.

She made her way to the store counter.

"Ready?" Uncle Henry was a handsome man. She'd never thought otherwise, from the moment she'd first laid her little girl eyes on him. But she could've been blind and still known that he was handsome—at heart. Next to Papa, Uncle Henry was the finest man she knew. She bit her cheek. Wallace James fell right alongside them.

Uncle Henry's eyes shone bright today. She reckoned she'd always recall when her uncle's light had gone out for a bit after his infant daughter had been born lifeless. Who could judge how a man reacts when a child dies?

"Yes. My coat is at Momma's desk."

———————◆•◆•◆———————

Maybe earlier thoughts of Uncle Henry were the cause of her sentimentality, but Clara found herself heading to the crepe myrtles rather than into the house when she arrived home. She stood at the family graveyard nestled among the trees.

Clara glanced down at the tombstones near her feet. *Samuel Benson Williams*. Her half-brother. Two other graves lay beside his. A stillborn cousin and, she smiled, the family pet. Although they were like grandparents to her, the Justices were buried near their own relatives at the local cemetery. Her Uncle Joe had died years ago in a prison cell. Clara conjured a shadowy image of him which drew feelings of disgust. Throughout her growing up, the name had rarely been mentioned. Joe had no grave in the family plots.

Her mind wondered to Wallace. Clara shuddered and pulled her coat more snug around her neck. The air now bit. *Wallace.* Was she fooling herself that he owned her heart as a brother or friend? Had the last year transformed his place in her heart to something deeper than brotherly affection? *Perhaps.* He'd never asked to visit her romantically, yet the tug between them pulled their interactions in that direction.

The uneven shuffling of footsteps let Clara know Papa was approaching. Injured in a train wreck years ago, Papa's limp produced a gait that was uniquely Ben Williams. Clara snuggled in as a strong arm enveloped her shoulders.

"You alright, Little Butterfly? You might get caught by rain."

Clara chuckled. "You've called me that name since I was a little girl. Seeing that I'm almost eighteen Papa, suppose we should find another word besides 'little' to describe me?"

She felt her father's smile spread as his chin rested atop her head.

"Well, then pick a word—precious, darling, lovely, bossy—and I'll do my best to use it."

"Hum. 'Bossy' is definitely not an option and the others are sweet, but on second thought, I'll stick with 'little.'"

"Too bad. I was feeling quite good about 'bossy.'"

"Papa!"

"Truth is, you are darling and precious and lovely, and you look just like your Momma."

Clara raised her head and turned to look him in the eye.

"The russet hair is Momma, but the face and smile are all thanks to you, Papa."

He winked.

"Back to my question. What's got you standing out here in the cold staring at graves? You alright?"

"Just feeling sentimental I suppose. Papa, truth is, I feel so sorry for Mary, losing her father and all. And now Maggie's father is so sick."

"Pastor Carlson just needs time to heal." He sighed. "Mason was the finest of men, and he's missed by lots of folks. Mary will make it through. It's the way of life—learning to live with death. At least here on earth. Separation can wound, but it doesn't have to destroy."

"You're a wise man, Papa."

"I'm a man who's learned a lot of lessons."

Clara shuddered again.

"Papa, I'm cold. Let's head inside before rain comes. What's Momma up to?"

The two of them turned toward the house, and Clara slid her arm through the crook at Papa's elbow.

"Your Momma was crumbling cornbread to make dressing when I walked out here."

Despite the cold air, Clara felt her face heat up. Cornbread dressing was reserved for special occasions.

"I hope she's using Aunt Lena's recipe." Momma had lots of talents, but cooking wasn't one of them, and she knew it.

Papa laughed along with her.

"Reckon Wallace likes cornbread dressing?"

"Papa, I happen to know he loves it."

"And I reckon he'd eat dirt if it was served up, as long as you are at the table."

"Papa! You're embarrassing me." Clara squeezed his arm.

The screen door squeaked as Papa pulled it back, opened the door, and motioned for Clara to walk through. The kitchen air warmed her cheeks. Her stomach growled.

"Smells good in here, Momma. How can I help?" Clara pulled open the oven door then eyed her mother. "Why don't you freshen yourself, then help me set the table. Lena and them will be here any second now." Momma put on her high falutin' voice. "We'll eat in the dining room tonight." The smile of a good-natured woman accompanied her words.

Clara felt her heart stir. Beautiful Momma. Russet curls, slightly grayed at the temples. Eyes that twinkled in the presence of Papa. Clara closed the oven door and began to move toward her bedroom. "I'll be back to help before you know it, Momma."

Papa' s voice stilled her. "The dining room?" Clara watched Papa move toward Momma. "I reckon I have to put on a tie."

"Don't gimme fits, Ben Williams. And get those boys of yours spruced up too. Years ago, you built me a fancy, big room to serve supper to a crowd, and a fancy room demands fancy clothes."

Clara smiled as Papa kissed Momma on the forehead. A peace tiptoed through her. How she adored her parents. Moments like this proved they were more than husband and wife. They were lovers. They were one another's closest companion. The uniqueness of each one came together and formed a beautiful being. Imperfect, but beautiful.

Clara's throat tightened. How she longed to be cherished the way Papa cherished Momma. Although he voiced his love for her unashamedly, its true revelation was in his eyes. Papa's eyes sparkled and their color seem to deepen with a glance or a gaze at Momma. Throughout her life, Clara had drawn comfort and contentment from that look in her Papa's eyes. Would any man gaze upon her in that same manner?

Wallace did.

"It's Dinner, Katherine. Not supper. A fancy room to serve dinner." Papa winked.

"Clara, don't set a place for your Papa. He'll eat leftovers alone in the plain kitchen."

Their three voices blended in laughter.

Clara moved to her bedroom and opened the door. Removing her coat she tossed it on the bed then made her way to the mirror and stared. Although Papa was a handsome man, and she did indeed look like him, Clara considered herself plain looking with no particular feature to draw one's eye, other than her angel kiss. She formed an opinion into a truth and accepted it. *Maggie is prettier than me. Does Wallace think so?*

Clara pulled at a curl resting on her shoulder, then twisted it around her finger. A thought occurred to her. Taking both hands, she pushed the hair above her shoulders and held it there, examining the reflection. Hum. Perhaps a short bob cut would be flattering. Would her shortened natural curls produce gentle waves or tight coils? She'd mention the idea of a short haircut to Momma and see how she responded.

The sound of Papa calling for her brothers startled her. Clara released her hair, slipped out of the uniform and moved to her closet.

She blew out a breath. Momma was cooking up something more than a meal, and most likely Papa and the guest of honor, Wallace, were helping her. Having him at their kitchen table over the years was not unusual, but tonight he was coming at Momma's insistence to join the entire family for dinner.

She stood before the mirror and dabbed a drop of cologne, and once again observed herself. The truth and depth of her dwelt within the display of her physical body. It was invisible to most eyes, but not to Wallace. He gazed into her soul.

Clara stared at herself and recalled Wallace's embrace in the graveyard months ago. His touch had comforted her, but not stilled her restlessness.

Indeed, her heart did not know how to feel about Wallace James.

Chapter 8

SEPTEMBER 1937 | LAYTON, TEXAS

Wallace found himself wiping moisture from his forehead. Despite the threat of rain and the cold September air blowing in through the open windows of his 1929 Plymouth, he felt perspiration on the back of his shirt collar. He blew out a long breath. Surely his aftershave would overpower the scent of his nerves.

He was proud of the green, used auto he'd bought from a flat broke customer and repaired to good working condition, but tonight the usual relaxation he found behind the wheel was gone. Nervousness had usurped it, and the pride he felt had nothing to do with his auto, but everything to do with an angel-kissed lady. Tonight he intended to declare his love to Clara Williams.

The one mile drive from the garage to her home was failing to ease his adrenaline. Fear was not a familiar feeling, and he shook his head to fight it, determined to be the victor. He had chosen to set aside the doubts that she wanted more than he could offer.

Wallace reached with his right hand and touched the bundle of writing tablets tied with a string next to him on the seat. "She'll love these." An unusual gift to lavish on most any other woman, but not his cherished Clara. He shook the memory of morning coffee with the Carlsons. They'd come upon him just as he was selecting the tablets, and he'd stuck them onto the nearest shelf as they approached.

The popping of gravel beneath his tires made him realize he'd turned onto the Williams driveway unawares. With the auto turned off, he grabbed the writing tablets and made his way to the front porch, protecting the tablets from the light drizzle. Thunder sounded in the distance.

He tugged the screen open then knocked on the wooden door. Laughter mingled with conversation seeped beneath it. Warmth greeted him as the door was opened.

"Wallace." Henry. A fine friend, but not the face he was hoping to see.

"Ev'nin'"

"Come on in and take off your coat. Ben's got a big fire going."

He sensed the weight of his coat—a type of armor protecting him in an environment that suddenly felt unfamiliar as though it were designed by dreams and imaginations in a place where reality ceased to exist. Wallace squeezed the package he held, a tangible reminder that he was no stranger to these walls and people. He pulled his coat from one arm, then the other and placed it in Henry's waiting hands.

Wallace noticed Clara's brothers and cousins playing a card game on the rug near the fireplace. "Howdy, boys." Tangled replies of "Howdy, Wallace," followed. "Supper will be ready soon," Ben spoke as he bent over the fireplace. Henry chuckled. "I wouldn't let Katherine hear you call it supper."

Wallace was glad to hear Henry's humor. Wallace had watched over the years as Lena cared for him during times his dark days took over. It was as though she were her his source of light. Their love seemed to be one of total abandonment for one another. He wanted that depth between him and Clara. With his love for her now unleashed, Wallace knew he would die for Clara, let alone devote himself to living for her.

Ben's eye met Wallace's when he stood and came to shake his hand.

"Excuse me, Wallace. *Dinner* will be ready soon." He watched Ben straighten his tie to validate his point.

"Dinner it is, and it smells mighty good." Wallace adjusted his own tie because his hands needed something to do. Mrs. Katherine's verbal invitation had clearly stated dinner, so he'd donned his best suit and tie—his only suit and tie—for the occasion. The older brother in a family where seven of the nine children were female, Wallace wore overalls working the family farm alongside his Pa and two older sisters. Ties and coats had been reserved for Sunday church, funerals, and weddings. He'd replaced his overalls with the Myers Garage uniform when he'd grown large enough to wear one at age fourteen.

Wallace took one of the open seats on the couch. Clara was a smart young woman. He had no doubt she surmised this evening held something in store other than a meal. He grinned. Was she feeling as strange as he in her own home?

Henry sat in a chair next to the fireplace. "Did you notice the article in the Herald this weekend about the continued decline in auto sales? Maybe we'll never open the used auto shop we daydream about." Wallace opened his mouth to reply just as Clara entered the room. His thoughts shifted.

She was beautiful. Her chocolate dress highlighted the russet curls resting below her shoulders, and he yearned to run his fingers through her hair. The hairstyle she'd chosen was one of his favorites on her — the front sides pulled up and clasped together in the back.

Holding the bundle that rested in his lap, he stood and made his way to her. He marked this moment, for at last, he removed the veil of friendship and allowed himself to gaze upon her as his future wife. He could have been eleven again and captivated by her for the first time. Desire suggested he pull her close and meld his mouth with hers. He supposed he should be thankful the room was filled with people to keep him proper.

"Wallace, I didn't hear you come in." Had she blushed?

"Evening Clara." He smiled. "I brought you a little something." He held the bundle toward her and she took it.

"Writing tablets. What a perfect gift." Her eyes met his. "I've almost used up my last one. Thank you." Her slender fingers drew the bundle to her chest.

"You're welcome."

"You haven't heard my newest story. It's as good as the grasshopper one. Maybe I can read it to you after supper." Supper. The verbal slip amused him.

Raymond interjected. "Is it the one about the lightning bug?"

"Yes, but keep it a secret, little brother."

"Wallace, it's my favorite of all of 'em."

"Well, if you like it that much, Raymond, I can't wait to hear it." Truth is, if Raymond or anyone else disliked the story, Wallace would still want to hear every word that Clara had pulled from her mind, formed into sentences, and tucked between a beginning and an end.

"Did Momma draw pictures for it, Clara?" Wallace glanced at Henry and Lena's youngest son."

"Not yet." Clara winked. "Maybe Uncle Henry will take his children to get ice cream at that new place in Greenville, and she'll have time to draw."

Wallace laughed out loud. His Clara was spunky. *His* Clara?

"Hey Papa, if Uncle Henry drives to get ice cream, can we go with them?"

"My children don't like ice cream, Raymond. They'd rather stay home and eat collard greens."

Amid youthful verbal denials and adult laughter, Wallace's eyes found themselves locked on Clara. He loved this family, but how he longed to have time alone with her. He had words of his own to share. Words that he hoped would begin the story of him and Clara. And a kiss. He had a kiss to share. Would she accept it? He'd be proper of course.

"Well," Clara grinned at him, "I came to say we would eat as soon as Wallace arrived, but since he's here…dinner is served."

Amid the clatter of silverware on plates and the chatter of people who knew one another well and loved each other deeply, Wallace bid his way through dinner bite by bite. Katherine had just mentioned clearing the table for dessert when Ben and Henry turned the discussion to state taxes. Clara began to twirl a lock of hair between her fingers. Though interested in the discussion, Wallace felt the corner of his mouth turn up. Clara must be bored.

The sound of an auto pulling onto the gravel drive quietened all conversation. Wallace heard car doors shutting. Ben made his way to the front room and soon the footsteps and voices revealed their owners. Garrett Forder, Mason's son and their state senator, stood in the dining room doorway behind Ben. Standing next to him was Mary and his young daughter Madie. Wallace blinked. Tall and thin, and the reflection of his father, Garrett's presence was almost startling with the recent passing of Mason.

Ben spoke. "Katherine, look who…"

"Mary!" Clara's greeting mingled with her father's as she jumped up from her chair then pulled her friend into a hug.

Seated beside the doorway, Wallace rose next to Clara and extended a hand toward the state senator who was nodding his greeting to the family. An honorable icon like his late father.

"I believe Ben was about to ask you to join us for dessert," Katherine's voice interjected.

As Wallace released his grip, he noticed Garrett plunge his hand into his coat pocket "Didn't mean to disrupt your dinner. We just stopped by with an invitation for Clara."

"For me?" Clara's eyes widened. A jolt went through Wallace as her fingers clasped his arm. Her touch was pleasant torment. He needed this woman to belong to him.

At Ben and Katherine's insistence, the party moved to the front room while Lena and Henry made their way to the kitchen to serve up dessert.

"After the special election in August," Garrett explained, "Congress has been called into another special session for a month. It begins September twenty-seventh."

"This about the amendment for the needy and teacher retirement?"

"That's right, Ben. The people of the great state of Texas are keeping us busy." Chuckles filled the air. "My wife, Cass, and I thought since my father's recent passing, it would be good to bring Mother and Mary along with us to Austin. We'll be leaving Monday."

Mary took up the explanation. "Garrett and Cass also offered for me to bring friends along." Wallace wrinkled his forehead. Mary's glance at him had been brief, but obvious. "So, Mr. Williams, Mrs. Williams, could Clara accompany us to Austin for a month as a gift from the Forder family? Of course, only if she wants to." Mary winked.

The entire room broke into vocal chaos as words of excitement collided with one another. Save one corner of the room where Wallace braced himself against the wall next to the clock. The ticking irritated him. He rubbed his temple. His hopes for a hasty courtship and rapidly approaching wedding were threatened should Clara agree to go. By her wide grin and flushed cheeks, he knew she had every intention of adventuring to the state capital.

More than a half hour passed while dessert mingled with details and trampled on his every nerve. Outside, a gentle rain had begun to fall, yet irritation seemed to form it into pelting sleet against his demeanor.

"And, Clara, guess what? Garrett knows a publisher there." Marys' statement settled on his shoulders.

"A publisher!" Wallace watched Clara's hands cover her mouth. Mrs. Williams gasped. Maybe becoming a famous author wasn't as farfetched as sweet Clara thought. He clinched his fingers against the potential rival named success, searching his heart for joy, but finding jealousy. How long had such wretchedness lay dormant in him?

"Yes! You should bring your favorite story with you. And the pictures too, if your Aunt Lena won't mind. Right, Garrett?"

"Right."

"Clara," Madie's high voice broke in. "You might get famous." The other young voices in the room agreed with Madie.

Wallace sipped his now tepid coffee. He couldn't compete with a publisher for Clara's immediate future. He grunted, enough that Ben turned and caught his eye. Twice Clara had looked at him, her face still flushed with excitement, yet her head tilted in question. His lack of enthusiasm must be apparent. With her third glance, he removed his wrist watch, the secret expression between them, encouraging her to take her time with the plans. The action teetered on hypocrisy. She rewarded the gesture with a smile. Gazing at her now, Wallace longed for the day when the secret expression between them was physical and intimate.

Relief swept through Wallace as the chatter of travel evolved into goody-byes filled with expectations for the departure only two days hence. Perhaps the hour wasn't too late for him to remain longer, so he made no attempt to leave. Lena had moved to stand next to him. She cleared her throat.

"Jacob and Raymond, how 'bout you two spending the night with your cousins." Wallace felt an elbow against his arm and looked down at Lena who raised her eyebrows. He saw Ben spring from his seat. "Katherine, let me help you in the kitchen." The woman of the house came and slid her hand in the crook of her husband's arm and headed toward the kitchen. It seemed Henry took up where Lena left off. "Youngins, first one out the door gets a dime." Hustle and bustle erupted.

The room cleared, leaving him alone with Clara.

"Mind if a stay a bit longer?" He moved to sit on the couch next to Clara, struggling to keep a respectable distance between them. Clara's hands went to her cheeks.

"Wallace, can you believe it? Mary inviting me to Austin. And, I might get to see a publisher."

"That sure is something. A month's a long time to be gone from home. Should you just send your story with Garrett?"

Clara moved her hands and grasped his forearms.

"Wallace, I'm not a homebody like Momma. I want adventure and to see places. Like Aunt Lena. And, like Papa." She released him.

"Seems to me, your Papa prefers to stay put."

"Only 'cause of Momma."

Wallace wasn't so sure. Many times while hunting, Ben had remarked on his traveling days working the railroad. There'd been no fondness in his words. But he wasn't here to argue with Clara. Indeed.

"I should be the one to show my work. And, imagine all the ideas I could get for new stories in Austin."

"Like what?"

She patted his wrist. "I don't know, but something fresh. New. Wallace, don't be an old fuddy-duddy. I thought you'd be excited."

He leaned back and laughed. "You called me 'old.'"

Her cheeks turned crimson, and the smile he gazed on in his dreams about did him in. Blood coursed in his neck. One hand grasped hers while the other rested against her angel kiss. This would be his moment. The trip to Austin. Her latest story. The voices wafting from the kitchen. The lateness of the evening. Nothing else mattered. His eyes were locked on hers.

"Clara, I love that you're an adventurer. I love that you write stories. I love that you're smart and sassy. I love how your russet curls lay over your shoulders. Since the day I first laid eyes on you, I've loved that you're kissed by an angel."

He saw her lips part as though she would speak. He moved his hand from her cheek to place a finger on her lips and hush her.

"I love you far more than a friend. I want you to be my wife. Soon. Very soon." He knelt on the floor in front of her, keeping hold of her hand. "Clara, let's get married. We can go to Austin later, as husband and wife." He kissed her fingers.

Tears began to drip from her beautiful eyes. His name slipped through her quivering lips as though it were air, so gentle, that the curls brushing against her shoulders created more sound.

His pulse accelerated.

Surely he'd misunderstood her answer.

Chapter 9

What was Wallace thinking? Clara slammed a fist into her pillow. The evening had opened a world of adventure to her, and she couldn't help but think that Wallace had closed it with his good intentions. His declaration of love and a marriage proposal had knotted her excitement and created an internal storm much like the thunder and lightning raging outside.

How pitiful the scene. The image of Wallace struck speechless, shaking his head as though he'd mistook her answer. He had not. The "no" had come out of hiding, trekking over her nerves and slipping through her lips. From where had it originated? Her head or her heart?

She groaned. Heaviness in her chest threatened her breathing. The pain of hurting Wallace felt unbearable.

Conversation with Momma and Papa had ushered in midnight and yielded little comfort. They spoke quiet words of understanding for her hesitation. *Hesitation?* The words they didn't voice spoke more loudly. Papa and Momma supposed their daughter was in love with Wallace James. *Am I?*

Her insides churned. Hadn't she hours earlier supposed herself to love him as a man? Had she not anticipated romantic intentions for the dinner? She'd seen the look in Wallace's eyes. The look Papa gave Momma. The look in Henry's eyes at the sight or mention of Aunt Lena. The look for which she longed. Rolling to her back, she kicked the covers, welcoming the cold air. Her skin tingled. She inhaled, willing herself to gather her emotions. *Dear God, settle my thoughts and show me what's happening inside my heart. Am I a fool?*

Wrapped in the darkness she examined her heart. Love for Wallace was there, and over the last few months she'd known it had ceased to be the love for a friend and become love for the man. Why had she said no? She *was* a fool. After all, wouldn't life with Wallace be an adventure all their own?

Yes.

Just not now.

"I'm supposed to go to Austin." Cold air formed her words into smoke that lingered before her. Traveling later with Wallace wouldn't get her a meeting with a publisher. Garrett Forder had to arrange that, and he was only in Austin every other year when the government was in session or for called sessions. No, the timing of this special trip was perfect.

Clara bolted upright. If Wallace had waited to declare his intentions, she would have responded differently. Her "no" was actually a "not now." A "yes, but not now." Because she couldn't manage her reasoning over her emotions at the time, answering "no" had seemed logical in the intensity of the moment. Clara felt a sense of relief and confidence. She'd misspoke her intentions. She knew she'd messed up things with him tonight, but tomorrow she would try to fix them. Wallace would surely understand.

Wrapped in fresh confidence and a quilt, Clara scurried to her parents' room and knocked on the door, bouncing to keep her feet warm on the cold floor. She needed to talk to them again.

"Momma? Papa? Can I come in?" Shuffling preceded the clearing of a throat. "Clara, come on in." Momma's voice. Clara bit her lip. Not since she was young had she knocked on her parents' door late at night. It opened with a squeak.

"Are you alright, Clara?"

"Yes, Momma." She moved to the edge of the bed, her eyes adjusting to the scene. Momma sat up with the covers pulled to her chin. Her long hair draping the arms of her gown. Only Papa's head shown as he lay there wide-eyed on his back.

"I figured something out and, I wonder what y'all think." The words felt stuck to her tongue. She worked to push them out.

"Tell us."

The next words gushed from her lips.

"I don't think I meant to say no to Wallace. I wanted to say 'not now.' I just want to go to Austin so much I couldn't think. So, tomorrow, I want to go tell him if he asks again, I'd tell him yes."

"Lands sake. She's just like her mother." Papa's declaration was accompanied by rolling to his side and shutting his eyes. Momma chuckled. A sudden recollection startled Clara, and similarities between past and present felt uncanny.

She and Momma had been gathering wildflowers for Aunt Lena's birthday, and ten-year-old Clara, eager for a good story, had asked how Papa and Momma fell in love. The story had included a detail that years since, watching her parents together, had slipped from the forefront of her memory. Momma had given Papa a no when he proposed. Said she was scared to get married.

"Later that day, I took off in the cart, hurrying to the train depot. Your Papa was leaving town, and I couldn't let him go without trying to fix things." Her words had drifted into a mumble. "Not that time." In this present sliver of time, Clara realized Momma had been voicing regret over their years apart.

The bed creaked as Momma leaned forward, patting her chest. The chuckle was gone. "Clara, you shouldn't trifle with his heart. If you're uncertain about Wallace, then think about letting it be for now. Don't give him hope if you might change your mind and snatch it back."

"But Momma, I can't imagine life without him."

"Clara, can you imagine marriage with him?"

She wiped hot tears from her cheeks. "Yessum. I mean, I think so."

Papa rolled back over and patted Momma's arm. "An uncertain yes is simply a no, Little Butterfly." He ran a hand over his face. "Can you imagine him married to someone else?"

"No, Papa. I ache when I think about that."

Momma looked at Papa, then cleared her throat. "If you talk to him tomorrow, be sure about your answer. And be ready to hear how he feels about your trip to Austin." She lay back down. "I will." Clara turned to leave the room, the weight of the quilt against her body. The weight of her decision against her heart. "I love you both. Night."

The confidence she'd displayed while heading to their room now felt like selfishness as she returned to her own. Clara slipped back into bed. "Ugh." The rumpled covers irritated her. The clock struck three. She moved to the kitchen.

Her breath shown in the moonlight slipping beneath the closed curtain. Perhaps it was the first rays of sun instead. In her befuddled state, hours had passed and the storm outside had eased back into a gentle mist. "I should light the stove." She sipped her coffee and coughed as the cold liquid attacked her throat. "And make more coffee." Empty coffee cups, Papa's wristwatch, and a wrinkled handkerchief on the table bore witness to conversation the night before. She slid to the end of the kitchen table bench and toward the wood burning stove. She arched her back, stiff from sitting for hours.

A wave of comfort whisked through her heart when she opened the stove door. Each night Papa made sure the stove was filled with wood for the next morning. Momma preferred the wood stove to the more modern gas stoves for heating the kitchen. She flicked some matches, and warmth greeted her. Soon the smell of fresh coffee filled the dim kitchen, yet when the clock announced the six o'clock hour, Clara was still the only one awake. A sigh escaped. Even the house seemed drowsy, stirring in the moments between night and dawn as light seeped beneath curtains.

Wearied, she reached for the coffee pot barehanded. "Ouch!" She poured a cup and continued her vigil. Her voice broke the silence of the hour. "Clara, grow up. Tell Wallace how you feel, and accept the outcome."

The clock chimed seven times. Momma appeared in the doorway, then came and pulled Clara to her. They shared the silence for a moment until Clara spoke against her mother's shoulder.

"Momma, why do two good things not feel good together?"

Momma sighed. "Well, I reckon one is good and one is best and that makes friction."

Clara pulled away to look her pretty mother in the eyes. "Momma, I remembered last night that you turned Papa down at first." Momma nodded. "Why?"

"Clara, like you, I was uncertain of what I wanted." Her head nodded back and forth. "No, I knew what I wanted, but was too scared to take the best being offered me. I've never been as brave as you are." Momma chuckled.

"I think you must have been brave for five years, while Papa was gone."

"If bravery is not a decision, but a means of surviving, then, yes, I was brave."

"What happened in those years?"

"Clara, perhaps it's time you know. Perhaps it's not. But either way, it's not my story alone to tell. And this is not the time. You have a decision to make. "

Clara kissed her Momma on the cheek. Momma wasn't shutting her out. She was being wise.

"Did you sleep?"

"No ma'am"

"Did you decide?"

"Yessum. I'll be honest with him and accept what happens." The coffee cup clinked as she sat it in the sink. "He opens the garage this morning, so I'll go before he gets busy."

"Do you want Papa to drive you? It's cold and moist outside."

"Not too cold to walk. I'll bundle up."

Momma moved toward the cooking stove. Gone were the days when Momma and Papa could make decisions for her. A longing for that childhood comfort pressed in. Clara reached for Momma and hugged her again, calmed by the motherly embrace. Clara inhaled the scent of lavender from her skin and hair. Momma had offered what she could by her words and her presence. The grown-up daughter knew she was on her own. "Thank you, Momma." Clara released her hold. "I best get a move on if I'm gonna see him before the garage opens."

A knock at the front door made Clara jump. She glanced at Momma who shrugged and began to move toward the front room. Papa's words halted her. "I'll answer it." He'd awakened.

"Momma, maybe it's Aunt Lena or Uncle Henry and something's wrong with the boys."

"Unless it's night, you know they knock as they're walking in. I reckon that'd surely be the case if something was wrong."

Speculation ceased before she drew her next breath.

Papa's voice. "Wallace."

Clara wrapped her clammy hand around her Momma's wrist. Her consumption of coffee threatened to rebel.

"I'm sorry, Ben. I know it's early. Before I open the garage," Wallace paused. Clara's eyes filled with warm tears. Did he regret coming?

"You want to see Clara?"

"Yes."

"Wait here."

Papa's uneven gait, more pronounced in the morning, drew closer until he stood to face her. His large fingers patted her shoulder. "Clara?" She felt her head nod back and forth and released Momma's wrist. A quick downward glance revealed that she was wearing her robe though she had no recollection of putting it on during her fitful night. There was nothing else to do but face the one who loved her. She moved to the front room, pulling the kitchen door closed behind her.

The sight of him, moistened by rain, made her catch herself in the doorway. How had she ever wondered whether she loved the man? Why had she wrestled a decision between him and a trip? Was she nothing more than a fickle, immature woman? The questions collided, and she drew in a deep breath to sort her answers. Yes, she wanted to marry Wallace James and give herself to him. Every fiber in her being felt the longing. If he asked her again this morning, no doubt she'd answer yes. Her stories could stay locked in her trunk for all she cared right now.

"Wallace." She moved next to him and reached to clasp his hand, but he made a motion to sit on the couch. Embarrassed, she sat and clasped her hands in front of her and stared at them. Sobs rose in her throat and she forced them down, though they clawed their way back up. She couldn't keep her composure. Tears dropped on her hands.

"Clara." Wallace sat down with his thigh against hers. His hand rested on her angel kiss. "Clara, I don't mean to make you cry. I came to apologize." His hand slipped away.

Her chest was heavy. It wasn't the hope of an apology that she'd spent the night working through. Indeed, the offering of an apology should come from her. She hoped the offering of another marriage proposal would come from Wallace.

"You don't have a reason to apologize." Her eyes met his, and their redness testified of his pain.

"I do. The supper visit was planned so I could come tell you how I feel. I figure you knew that." A weak smile spread on his lips.

"I suspected." She returned a smile.

"So, when the Forders came and invited you to Austin, and even mentioned you might meet a publisher, I felt mad. I'm ashamed to say, it, but it's true. "

"Wallace,"

"Please let me finish. So, I thought more about myself than the situation you were in." He took her hands. "I shouldn't have asked to marry you." His leg began to shake against her own. Bile rose in her throat. Was he regretting his offer or just the timing of it? He squeezed her fingers. "I should've waited." Her body relaxed. She captured her emotions and separated the little girl in her from the young woman, allowing the elder to speak.

"It's the opposite. I owe an apology." His leg stilled. "I made the mistake. When the moment was in front of me, I didn't see it for what it was."

He blew out a breath. "You didn't think I was proposing?" Sensing frustration from the mild tempered man before her, she locked her fingers with his.

"Yes, I recognized the proposal." Pulling their entwined hands toward her face, she wiped her wet cheeks against his skin. "But I didn't see that it was what I wanted more than anything else in life." An urging built inside her. "More than an adventure to a city or a printed story. Wallace, ask me again, Right here. Right now."

His fingers slid from hers. As his hands made their way to her cheeks, she shivered. Her lips were tingling, eager for the question and the kiss she anticipated.

"Clara." His eyes darkened. "No. not right now. You go to Austin free as a butterfly."

Confusion and embarrassment rushed in forcing quick breaths. "But, Wallace"

"I'll be here when you come back." He removed his hands and she missed them. Hers trembled.

"Wallace?"

"I simply came to say I was sorry. Clara, I know you right well. I know you've wrestled. Go on your trip. No tellin' what's in store for you."

His decision was right. After hours of wrestling to make her decision how could his be right? But it was. The realization forced her to sit back. Was this relief? No, it was hope. She could go without him then return home to him — maybe even as an author. He was giving her the adventure she longed for, an opportunity to ease her curiosity, and see life beyond the familiar. If she saw his words as anything but a delay, then she'd go crazy. Perhaps she already had.

"You would do that? You would wait for me without a promise between us?"

"Like I said, I'll be here when you get back."

He stood. "Now, since you leave Monday morning, I reckon you got lots to do." He moved to the front door. Was this his goodbye? She sprang from the couch and grabbed at him. He stilled. She wrapped her arms around his neck, her body still longing for the kiss she'd never felt. He didn't respond.

"Will you write to me?"

"Do you have an address?"

"No"

He smiled. "Then you write to me first." He pulled away, and her arms fell to her side.

"Wallace, can we kiss good-bye?"

His face gathered into a grimace. Was her boldness inviting or insulting?

"I'd like nothing better than to kiss you. And if you were rightly mine, I would. But you're not."

He stepped to the door and opened it, then pushed the screen to walk out. Her feet felt heavy. Her legs weak. He glanced back her way. "You travel safe, Clara. And have fun." He walked out and down the steps. She forced movement toward the doorway.

"'I'll see you at church tomorrow."

He answered without turning. "I won't be there."

She'd never known Wallace to skip church for any reason other than sickness. He was avoiding her.

Clara felt the sting of being set aside and recognized the irony of that emotion.

She now understood how she'd made him feel.

Chapter 10

"You cain't hide any longer." His Pa's tall figure filled the doorway of the home where Wallace had grown up. Wallace felt a smile spread across his lips, despite the heaviness weighing on his body and spirit. "You got to try and get on with living. Time will tell you about Clara." Wallace knew his Pa spoke truth. Pony James had always been straightforward with him. "Yessir, I know that." Ma slipped under Pa's arm braced against the doorframe. Wallace wrapped his arms around her stout figure. He'd gotten his height from Pa and his broad shoulders from Ma. He'd gotten his strong faith from both. "Bye. I'll be back next weekend or at least see you at church Sunday."

Thunder sounded in the distance and the light sprinkle that he'd combated while loading the auto morphed into heavy rain as he sprinted down the porch steps. He dashed to his auto and slipped inside. Running one arm across his face to dry it, he started the auto with the other. He waved goodbye to the comfort and footing he'd found at home, hoping he'd arrive in Layton with them intact.

The moment he walked away from Clara Saturday morning, he knew he couldn't bear to see her the next day in church. When he'd closed the garage Saturday night, he'd gathered a few belongings and headed home to Evan, an hour's drive, to stay at his parent's farm. The garage was closed on Monday, and for the first time he could recall, he'd skipped being at a Sunday church service. He'd hidden out for two days. His family had done the same, and that had both surprised and soothed him. He'd been a grown man in need of Ma and Pa.

With caution he eased into the memory of his last encounter with Clara. "I won't be there." He replayed the words aloud, feeling each syllable. Those were his last spoken words Clara would carry with her to Austin. Would they shout above the truth spoken before them—that he'd "be here" when she returned? His memory of driving back to the garage after the encounter was as foggy as the weather before him now. He did recall throwing his body onto the small bed of his side room in the garage and weeping the unfamiliar sound of a soul ripping from its body.

Layton appeared in the distance against the flat Texas terrain. Time to face his day to day life and the remaining people who filled it. His homegrown footing seemed to slip a bit. He pulled onto the garage lot, turned off his auto. Uncertainty opened the auto door for him.

"I'm soaking wet." Wallace wrestled to slide the key into the door of Myers Garage while jostling a bag of clothes and another bag of food. Heaviness clung to him. He shook his body to release loose water from his clothes. What he'd give to shake the heaviness.

The lock released, and Wallace tossed the key on the shelf beside the door then set the bags on the floor. He tugged on the light string hanging from the ceiling in the middle of the room. The garage office was so small that he needn't take a step to yank the light on. A single light bulb shone in the center of the room and created shadows in the corners. Wallace inhaled. The smell of motor oil and rubber tires was familiar and soothing.

He'd spent the last two days mulling over himself. The truth was simple. He ran a garage and enjoyed it. He was a man of tools and grease. He'd never be a man of paper and ink. He glanced at his calloused hands. Would they be enough to hold her? Did Clara love him or just his familiarity? "Time will tell." Pa's words replayed in his mind.

Wallace wouldn't enter a marriage empty-handed. With no one but himself to look after and having a free room in the back of the garage as part of his pay, he'd managed to set aside a sum of money over his years, though he'd lived on a portion of it during the hardest part of the Depression when the auto repair business had practically come to a halt. After the owner took his fifty percent of labor charges, Wallace had split his earning forty-sixty with his mechanic at the time, but not taken from him in return.

Despite that practice, the amount he'd added to his balance in the last three years gave promise of buying the small house Ma's cousin had vacated on the edge of town. Maybe in a couple more years, he could spare enough to open a used auto store next to the garage. He and Henry had dreamed of such during the worst of the economy. It had been a way of staying hopeful for the future.

A mouse scurried across his foot. "Still ain't caught?" He glanced at the trap in the right corner. The alluring cheese was missing. "Smart critter." For three months the thing had avoided being trapped. Lifting the bags, he stepped toward his room and pushed the door open with his foot. He eyed the jar of Aqua Velva on the bedside table and smirked. No need to wear it while Clara was gone. Maybe he wouldn't even bother to shave. He stacked three jars of home canned apples on his small shelf next to his two plates and bowls. Clara called them sets.

He shivered. "Light the stove, Wallace." He smirked at his habit of talking out loud to himself. With warmth feeling the room, he stripped off his wet shirt and slipped into his uniform, a light blue shirt with his name sewn on the pocket. A knock at the door startled him. The garage didn't open for another hour. He tucked the last of his shirt into his pants. "Lands sake, I'm coming." His feet pounded the short distance to the door, then he yanked it open. Dread pressed in. The last person he'd want to see this morning stood before him with water dripping from his face. Wallace felt his homegrown footing flee.

"Ben." He couldn't recall never wanting to see his friend until this moment. "Get in." He stepped aside to allow Clara's father entrance. *Friendship.* Had he lost that too? If Ben had a bone to pick, he'd be standing up for Clara. Wallace didn't welcome the awkwardness he felt. Ben removed his coat and hung it on a hook.

"Auto trouble?"

"Naw. I'm here for other reasons."

Reasons? More than one.

"I was gonna brew some coffee. If you don't mind bitter, you're welcome to a cup." Wallace reached for the percolator and noticed his hand shaking.

"I'll brew it. Can't stand bitter coffee." Ben grabbed the appliance from his hand and offered a smile that was far from the sarcasm in his voice. Wallace leaned against the desk, unable to arrange words into thoughts. Ben must have understood, for he kept talking.

"Missed you at church Sunday."

"Never skipped before."

"I reckon I understand." His friend moved to stand beside him. "She missed you being there." Wallace delved into his discomfort and embraced the conversation.

"I figured she needed to chatter about her trip and say her goodbyes without my shadow over her. We both needed that." Wallace cleared his throat. Questions stumbled over one another in his thoughts. How is she? Did she go? Did I hurt her much? Does she hate me? Without a pause he asked the question that enveloped them all. "Did she tell y'all much?"

"I suspect she told her Momma and me just about everything. "

"I shouldn't have asked her to marry me when I did."

"Maybe. Maybe not."

"When she told me she changed her mind—did she tell you that?" Ben nodded his head back and forth. "When she changed her mind, I already knew that she needed time, even if she didn't think so."

The coffee stopped percolating, and Ben took a cup from the desk and filled it, extending it to him. Wallace clasped his hands around the warmth and watched Ben fill a cup for himself.

"She'd been up all night, trying to figure out her heart."

Wallace groaned. Tears fell unsolicited from his eyes. Shame on him for hurting her.

"Now, Wallace, let me finish. I love my girl. I'd die for her. But, considering every part of this tangled mess, I'd say you made a good decision not proposing again in the moment." His friend slurped a drink. "Pains me to say it, though."

"I reckon it helps me to hear it."

"Katherine insisted I find out how you're doing. We're both worried about you."

"I ran every minute of our talks through my mind over and over until I felt crazy. I couldn't undo the asking and save it for later, so I did the best I knew to do and give her time. Truth is, Ben, if I ever had her, I'm scared I lost her."

"Not if she really loves you."

"Which is the only reason she should marry me. Not friendship. Not expectations. Certainly not guilt or pity."

Wallace placed his cup on the desk. The coffee wasn't setting well.

"We hold nothing against you, Wallace. Nothing against Clara neither. We know the pain of knotted up lovers."

Wallace knew little about Katherine and Ben's history other than they'd had time apart. Whatever the scenes had been, their plot had evolved into the beautiful story he knew.

"Thank you." Wallace extended his arm to Ben and shook the hand of his friend then addressed him as such.

"Reckon she'll get a story published?"

"Wouldn't that be something."

"Did Pastor Carlson preach Sunday?"

"No, he was there, but still too weak to do anything but sit amongst his people. That burst appendix about did him in."

"Who preached?"

A chuckle rose from Ben. "You're lookin' at him."

"That right?" Wallace returned the chuckle. "Hate that me and my folks missed that."

"Truth is, that's leads me to the other reason I'm here."

"You want me to start preaching?" Wallace laughed.

Ben's head shook side to side as he paced the few steps back and forth in the small office, his gait leaving an uneven rhythm. Wallace realized Ben was troubled. "It seems Henry's goin' dark again."

Wallace shoved his hands into his pocket. As far as he knew, Henry hadn't gone dark, as his family referred to his mood change, in over five years. He listened as Ben described Lena's panic yesterday morning when Henry refused to leave the house to go run the business.

"Maggie stepped up to help yesterday." A pain ran through Wallace at Ben's words. It would have been Clara to step in had she'd not left for Austin. No doubt, she would have never gone had she any hint of Henry's struggle. The man had seemed fine three nights ago.

"With Mason passed and Garrett gone, I feel responsible for the businesses until Henry gets alright."

"I'll check on Maggie a couple times today. I can work Mondays if it comes to that."

"Took the words right from me. I'd be obliged. Katherine will be in to check the books and place any orders. Mrs. Wilton is gonna come cook in Lena's absence at the diner. She won't leave Henry."

"Reckon this will be a short spell for him?"

"I pray it will. Not sure what triggered it. But Lena and the Lord is what will get him through it."

"Should Clara be told?"

"I don't think so."

With that, he watched Ben slip into his coat and push open the door. The man had a job to get to. Rain blew inside the office, forming small puddles of mud on the floor. Wallace reckoned he should sweep. With the slam of the door behind him, he gathered the set of mugs and washed them in the small sink. A glance at the clock told him the garage was already open for business. His current mechanic was late.

He dried the mugs with a clean rag then opened the cash register, trying to ignore the question nagging at him.

How had he managed to pick the father of the woman he loved as his good friend. He'd either have them both or lose them both. Wallace was no fool. Ben's loyalty, if pulled, belonged to Clara.

Chapter 11

Clara didn't care if she ever sat in an auto again. It was lunchtime Tuesday. An afternoon yesterday and a morning today on the road and her rebellious body was behaving as though it'd traveled nonstop for days. Clara pulled herself from the back seat of Garrett Forder's Cadillac. She and Mary had traveled by auto with him. Cass, Madie, and Mrs. Forder were due to arrive on the train this afternoon.

Clara stretched. The house before her was modest but welcoming just as Mary had described it the night before at the motel in Waco. "I wish I could move Garrett's little house to Layton and live in it. It would be divine for starting a family." Despite a deliberate smile, Clara's face must have shown her sadness at the mention of starting a family, for Mary had immediately grabbed her hand and squeezed it. "Cheer up, Clara," her tone hopeful, "and remember that Wallace must want you to enjoy your trip. Why else would he have turned you down?"

The memory of those words made Clara roll her eyes even as she stood now rubbing her back. Sweet Mary, often diluting her intended encouragements with misspoken words. Clara had long grown to overlook that fault about her friend and appreciate her true intent.

Clara smiled. Her heart was filled with fondness for the Forder family. Their home in Layton was a mansion centered on their estate and gave nary a hint of its generous, down-to-earth inhabitants who mingled in the humble homes of their friends.

Clara felt a grin spread across her face. Yes, the Forders were wealthy and lived a wealthy lifestyle, yet they were generous to the community, their employees, and their friends. Over the years Papa spoke about how well he was paid. She reckoned Uncle Henry was paid well too.

She suspected the Austin abode was a type of dollhouse for Mary. Clara had learned far more about it than she ever would have thought to ask. Mary rattled off details as they'd lain talking in their beds last night. Clara had forced her eyelids open and listened. The house had a front room, a small dining room, a kitchen, an indoor bathroom, and three bedrooms. The yard was small and vacant of trees. Mary had gone on to explain that the Forders rented out the house in the year the state legislature didn't meet. Otherwise, it sat vacant after the biennial session, cared for by Cibby and her husband George who were caretakers during the Forder's absence. Cibby and George lived next door.

Garrett began handling the suitcases. Mary's hand wrapped around Clara's arm and bid her toward the front porch. "Isn't it as adorable as I described?" Clara squeezed Mary's hand. "More so." Indeed, Clara found that she was excited to step inside the doors to her new home for the next four weeks, although an image of her true home marched to the front of her mind,

So little and so much could happen in a month's time. Would she find Raymond and Jacob changed in appearance when she returned? The thought of not hearing Momma and Papa's voices for that long made her throat tighten. Perhaps she could arrange a time to call the Justice Store and talk to them. For all his indulgences toward their comfort, out of respect for Momma's wishes, Papa still hadn't bought his family a telephone.

And Wallace? She had never gone this long without being in his presence, taking in his words, inhaling his scent. She was a heart divided. Rather than be stranded in homesickness, she chose to romp in the adventure ahead and focus on what lie in front of her.

A scent she didn't recognize welcomed her as she stepped through the doorway. "Smells so good." Mary released her and moved to pick up a small white bowl on a table. It overflowed with various dried flowers, leaves, and fruits. "It's Cibby's own concoction. Isn't it delightful? Peach, apple, basil, plumeria, and who knows what else."

"Did I hear my name?"

Clara turned to see a tall, slender woman standing in the doorway.

"Cibby." Mary bounded over and hugged her.

"My goodness, Mary, you've grown into a beautiful young woman since I last saw you." Clara smiled. Mary was beautiful. The two embraced as Cibby shared condolences. Clara was uncomfortable intruding on the private moment. She remained quiet, still unsure how a person lived after a loved one died. Mary pulled away from the embrace. Her eyes met Clara.

"Cibby, meet Clara Williams. My dear, dear friend."

"Another beauty. Welcome to Austin." Clara felt her smile spread from cheek to cheek.

"Thank you. I feel like I'm dreaming just bein' here."

"You ladies surely didn't pack like this is a dream." Garrett lumbered through the door with a suitcase in each hand and one tucked beneath an arm. Moisture shown on his brow while a grin shown on his lips. He set the cases on the floor while he and Cibby exchanged hellos mingled with condolences and instructions.

"Mr. Forder, I have lunch on the stove and just put supper in the oven. I figured y'all might want to eat before going to the train station. There's plenty for the Mrs. Forders and Madie too. I also figured Cass might appreciate not having to cook supper. Of course, I hope I didn't spoil any dinner plans."

Clara's stomach growled on cue. Cibby smiled. "I'm glad my efforts won't go to waste." She moved to the door after kissing Mary on the cheek. "Enjoy Austin, Clara." She slipped away.

Clara turned to Mary and bounced on her toes, prompting Mary to pull her down the hall. A gasp unbefitting a young woman escaped Clara. The bedroom was beautiful.

Clara dried the last plate from supper while considering the scenes and people of the household. How strange to mingle as family with the Forders. Unlike the large layout of their Layton home, these small rooms invited intimacy and afforded her a closeness that bordered on the edge of awkwardness. Voices floating from one room into the next. Bath water running in the tub. Bedroom doors closing. She supposed the brevity of her visit thus far lent itself to her sense of intruding. Her mind knew the truth was quite the contrary. She was wanted here. The Forder's generosity and graciousness were meant to be embraced.

Mary stood beside her washing the final serving dish, and Madie arranged flatware in a drawer. Garrett, Cass, and Mrs. Forder could be overheard unpacking and setting up their rooms. Madie pushed the drawer closed and it shook Clara from her thoughts. "I'm going back to our room and set up my books and toys." The young girl brightened a place with her presence. "It's gonna be fun sharing a room. Y'all come there when you finish." Clara turned in time to see Madie bound through the doorway. "Madie," Mary spoke up, "don't forget that your tutor is dropping by tonight." The eight-year-old feigned a whine. "Why do I have to do school every day when we're on vacation." Mary retorted. "You're not on vacation. And you can't just stop going to school." Mary looked at Clara. "Garrett figures a tutor is better than sending her to a new school.

Clara felt herself looking forward to time with Madie. Perhaps being around the child would ease the lonesomeness for her brothers and cousins. The presence of busyness might shadow the absence of Momma and Papa. Clara could think of nothing desirable enough to mask the void of Wallace. A restlessness to write home hovered inside.

"Life with Madie is never dull," Mary giggled and slipped the last dish into the cupboard. Clara put away the dishtowel. "I like that about her." She glanced at the dining room. All was in order. "Well, shall we go to our room and see what Madie has in store for us?" Her arm linked with Mary's as they moved through the house.

No sooner had Clara sat on the small bed she'd be using when Madie came to her holding a small leather-bound book.

"Clara, guess what this is." Madie turned to Mary. "Don't tell her." Clara's guesses proved incorrect. Madie giggled. "Give up?" Clara feigned surrender and shook her head. The book was placed on Clara's lap and opened to the front page. A disproportioned drawing of a yellow flower stared up at her. Clara's hand covered her heart as a resemblance set in.

"Is this your special drawing book?"

"Yes. One time, Mary told me you and your Aunt Lena drew butterflies in a book for special reasons. So, I'm doing that with flowers. Do you still have your butterfly book?"

Clara felt heat rise to her cheeks. Not only did she still have it, she'd brought it with her. "Your book is beautiful," her fingers thumbed the pages, "and yes, I have my book. Go open my drawer in the dresser." Clara winked. Madie gasped and darted to the dresser. "I brought it because it inspires me when I write."

With the three of them seated on her bed, they looked through both books. "Clara, show me a really, really special one." Clara turned to the drawing of a red butterfly and pointed. Madie's voice read the name on the picture. "Papa." The letters were large and misshaped. Clara glanced at Mary who already knew the meaning of the drawing. "Yes, I drew that red butterfly when I was five to show how much I love my Papa." Madie's fingers slid across the drawing. "It's pretty."

Her hands flipped to the last page. Madie noted that the page had two butterflies on it. Clara rolled her eyes. She'd not get out of explaining "Wallace and Clara."

A knock on the door drew Madie's attention from the books. Clara relaxed at the change of focus. Garrett and Cass passed by the bedroom door and soon a welcome was overheard.

"Andrew. Good to see you. Come in."

A groan escaped Madie, and she slid off the bed. Mary must have sensed her curiosity, for Clara looked up to see her mouthing the word tutor. Cass appeared in the doorway. "Madie, Mr. Slayton is here to talk about school. Come greet him." Mister?

Clara could hear the guest speaking, and the high voice floating in air sounded young. The tone was respectful, yet confident. Mr. Slayton was not the old spinster Clara had imagined as a tutor. This revelation might explain why Mary was checking herself in the mirror and adjusting her hair. Clara muffled a chuckle as she put away her butterfly book. Following Mary out the door, she afforded herself a glance as she passed by the mirror. After all, she wasn't meeting an old spinster.

Indeed. The image before was like none she'd ever seen. Clara nudged Mary with her elbow. She suspected his height exceeded Wallace's six-foot-four by two inches. Though disguised behind full slacks and a shirt, his arms and his legs seemed as thin as her own. Resting atop competent shoulders was a genteel face embellished with wire-rimmed glasses and hair as black as the Texas earth, swooped to one side and apparently governed by hair tonic. His skin was pale. Did the man never spend time outdoors? Clara detected a hint of an all too familiar aftershave. The scent belonged to Wallace.

"Mr. Slayton," Garrett extended his arm toward Mary and her, "you may recall my sister Mary."

"Hello, Mary. Good to see you again."

"Likewise, Andrew."

Clara noted Mary's smile. It was her familiar, unpretentious one. No hint of flirtation in the way she spread her lips. The introduction made it obvious she'd met the tutor before, and despite the glimpse in the mirror, her lack of chatter about the man indicated she had no romantic interest in him.

"And, this is her dear friend from home, Clara."

Had the guest blushed?

"It's a pleasure to meet you, Clara. Welcome to Austin."

She nodded her head. "Thank you. It's nice to meet you too."

"Clara," Garrett interjected, "Andrew is a student at the university here. His father is a professor who also served in the state senate alongside the current governor."

"What do you study there?" She bit her lip, hoping she'd worded the question properly.

"Mathematics. I enjoy numbers. I plan to teach."

Mrs. Forder appeared and greeted the guest with familiarity on her way into the kitchen. Mary nudged Clara in that direction. "We'll help Mother with coffee while you all talk business."

Andrew cleared his throat. "While you are all present in the room, I want to extend my condolences in person over the passing of Mr. Forder. I will miss my hearty discussions with him when he came to visit."

"Thank you, Andrew." Mrs. Forder, who had paused in her mission, squeezed the man's hand. Clara noted his slender fingers and well-groomed nails. She curled her own into the palms of her hands, noting the uneven edges. Maybe she'd file them and beg some red nail polish from Mary. Adorned nails somehow hadn't mattered at home.

When the business of the evening ended, three of the five females excused themselves to various tasks. Clara followed Mary's lead, remaining in the company of Garrett and the tutor.

"Andrew." A sense of awkwardness formed a knot in Clara's stomach as Mary's eyes implored her. What is this dear friend up to? "Clara is a writer." Clara's knotted stomach plunged to her feet. Was this man also the publisher? Mary and Garrett should have prepared and primped her.

"A writer?" Andrew's question was addressed to Clara. "Of what sort?" Blast you, Mary. I'll plot revenge. Clara cleared her throat. "I write stories for children."

"How fascinating. An author. You obviously enjoy words." A broad smile supported the ones he spoke. "Would I know of your stories?"

Thoughts of shaving Mary's gorgeous locks appealed to Clara.

"Oh, surely not. They are a hobby at best. And I am writer, but not an author."

"You mean to say your stories are not published?" He leaned forward in his chair, closing the gap between their two seating places.

"Yes." Her tongue tangled. "I mean, no, they are not published."

"We plan to introduce her to a publisher while she is visiting. You should read the story she brought with her. It's delightful." Mary's words were sweet with sincerity, making it difficult for Clara to imagine her bald. He was not the publisher. Relief set in.

"May I?"

Only after I shave Mary's head. "If you'd like."

"I would."

Surprising herself, Clara glanced at Garrett for support. She supposed he was the nearest semblance of the men from whom she drew courage—Papa, Uncle Henry, and Wallace. He nodded his encouragement.

"Alright, then. Excuse me." She rose and made the unsought trek to the bedroom.

She was surprised to see Andrew stand as she returned to the room. The lined papers clothed in her penmanship and tied together with ribbon felt like a meager offering as she released them into his open hand.

His brows wrinkled, then he seated himself and released the ribbon. Clara turned to leave the room, lest she pass out. Andrew's voice stopped her.

"No, stay. Please." Clara plopped onto her chair as though she were a sack of potatoes. The Forders sat in silence. Tortuous silence. Clara stared at Andrew as his eyes moved from right to left, and his hands slid one page behind another. The final pages were Lena's illustrations.

At last Andrew looked her in the eye. "Nice title."

"Thank you."

He straightened the papers and began to tie the ribbon. "It's a modest start."

Beside her, Mary sighed.

Clara controlled her trembling, but her tongue paid the price. She tasted blood. "Yes, well, as I said, I'm a writer. Not an author." She stared at her knees. Andrew Slayton needs to scat.

"No, Clara. I didn't mean to insinuate that your writing was modest. I'm an idiot. Forgive me." He stood. "I meant to say the handwritten pages are a modest start for getting published." He moved to stand in front of her. Clara's breathing was shallow. "The story is delightful. I wonder if you would allow me to type it for your presentation. Your illustrations could be presented as they are."

Clara raised her head and met Andrew's eyes. His lips were spread in a smile. "I can't pay you." He handed the papers to her. "I don't want pay. It would be an honor." She returned his smile. "Then, yes. I'd be honored in return."

His slim frame rose to full height, and he offered his hand to pull her up. The only other hands of a grown man she'd held belonged to Papa and Wallace. Those were hands of industrious, serving men. The hand grasping hers now was soft as though it had been served and never had need of labor. The touch renewed her belief that her hands belonged to the young man in Layton. "If the Forders don't mind, I can stay after my tutoring session tomorrow. I should finish in no time at all."

"Stay." Mary's voice scattered the tension. Garrett stood and extended his arm to Andrew. The soft hand released Clara's own, and the party moved to the door. "Good evening." Andrew spoke as he walked out the door, then turned to give Clara a nod.

The evening's potential invited itself into the writer from Layton, brushing her homesickness as it nestled in.

Chapter 12

Clara stifled a yawn as she slipped her change and the hotel postcard into her handbag. This Friday had begun at five in the morning in Austin when she rose to prepare her suitcase for the weekend San Antonio shopping and sight-seeing adventure. Standing in the lobby of the grand Menger Hotel, she found herself surrounded by tall white pillars, patterned tiles, and walls painted in soothing pastels. Luxury to the girl from Layton.

Mary had informed her once she wrote her note on the postcard, she could pay the desk clerk for postage and be assured the card would go out with the afternoon mail. She imagined Momma and Papa surrounded by Aunt Lena, Uncle Henry, and all the youngins, admiring the scene on the postcard. A hint of regret pinched her heart that a postcard would arrive before a letter. She would have written sooner had the Forders not kept her so busy. It had been all she could do to get a letter off to Wallace.

The thought of him conflicted her. She missed his voice and the comfort of his familiarity. Yet, the longing for him eased in the presence of Andrew, whose obligations as a tutor made him present every day this week. And that presence had accompanied them to San Antonio in place of Garrett and his family when Madie fell ill the night before last.

Andrew mingled among the white pillars. She need only turn to see his lean figure. Clara resisted the urge to do so. Instead, she adjusted her handbag, took a mint from the crystal bowl on the registration desk and went to stand next to Mary who rested on a large ornate bench.

Her stomach roared as though she'd never fed it. Clara covered her middle with her hand, knowing the touch wouldn't quieten the growl. Goodness, must it make such a commotion. Clara rolled her eyes when Mary turned to face her with a chuckle.

"I'm hungry too."

"So am I, dear." Mrs. Forder turned from the registration desk and came to stand beside them. "As soon as Andrew returns, we'll freshen up then eat lunch. He escorted the baggage clerk to the auto." Clara clasped the hand

Mrs. Forder extended toward her and felt herself drawn against the dear woman's side. "Then, our adventure begins. How I wish your Momma were here with us." Warmed by Mrs. Forder's generosity, Clara felt the words press against her heart just before a grin spread on her lips. Momma had a natural elegance that thrived in Layton and suited the limited adventures life brought her there. Indeed, Momma would prefer to experience San Antonio in her kitchen through the pastel photograph on the postcard rather than in person.

Clara noticed Andrew coming back through the lobby front door. He came to stand beside Mary. "Ladies, your bags are being delivered to your room. I will gladly escort you there." That said, Clara followed Mary and her mother to the second floor with Andrew a pace behind her, but close enough that his hand pressed against her back, sending a tingle down her spine. Up to this moment that sensation had been loyal to Wallace. Clara didn't know what to think about its mutiny. Andrew was bold.

Russet curls lay scattered on the checkered tile floor. Panic surged through Clara for a moment. Had she allowed any semblance of natural beauty to be snipped away? She lifted her fingers, now freshly painted the color of cranberries, and ran them beneath her short locks. She'd gazed in the mirror as the metamorphosis took place, looking away now to observe the abandoned locks. Clara lifted her eyes back to the reflection in the mirror and grinned. The brief doubt fizzled.

She'd ventured where only curiosity had gone before. Not always a good decision, she realized, but harmless when it came to hair. Her eyes, cheeks, and angel kiss fared well in the risk, for their display had brightened and enlarged beneath the short bob. Adrenaline skipped through her. Clara admired what she saw. She leaned down and gathered a lock for a keepsake. An image of Wallace darted through her mind. Perhaps he'd fingered this very lock.

Her admiration was interrupted when Mary squealed in the salon chair to her right. "You're as cute as a bug's ear." Clara winced. Mary chuckled. "I was being silly. Seriously, Clara, you're beautiful. The stylish haircut is perfect for you." Clara relaxed, then winked at herself in the mirror. "I am quite the looker now." Heat hit her cheeks, and a giggle made its get away.

Their salon appointments behind them, the three ladies made their way down the sidewalk to their hotel lobby where Andrew stood waiting, ready to escort them to their first stop on the shopping trip. Clara met his gaze.

"You've cut your hair." He cleared his throat.

Obviously. "Actually, the beautician cut my hair."

He blushed. Had she offended him? She'd only meant to tease.

"Of course. The beautician." He took a step toward her. "I hardly recognized you."

She dare not mention her embarrassing angel kiss that would make her recognizable no matter the hairstyle. Perhaps Andrew hadn't noticed it. No, most likely he was too polite to say that he had. Then again, he had touched her back. Maybe politeness wasn't what tied his tongue about the mark. Did it bother him the way it bothered her? Unlike the way it didn't bother Wallace at all.

Mary and Mrs. Forder faced Clara. Their raised eyebrows, like mother like daughter, hinted at their amusement.

"Hum. I wonder what that says about my old look. No need to answer. I'd rather not know."

Goodness, she felt embarrassed by her spunkiness.

His smile sent a twinge to her heart.

"It says that lovely became more lovely."

Her spunkiness was tongue-tied and could only offer a smile. To Andrew's credit, he didn't pause before she heard him address her companions.

"And, Mary and Mrs. Forder, you both look lovely. Always. Are we ready to depart?

Depart? Clara grinned. She'd been ready to simply leave.

Andrew Slayton was proving to be quite intriguing.

Clara followed Mrs. Forder's suggestions when it came to selecting the clutch and shoes to match her gown for the governor's birthday party they would attend. After all, she had no idea what her evening gown looked like. Mrs. Forder had pre-ordered dresses for all four Layton ladies attending the governor's party on Tuesday, and insisted that the stop at Frost's Department Store to pick them up be the last one of the shopping spree. Clara couldn't imagine the Joske's store they were in now not having evening gowns. Then, who was she to question Mrs. Forder's plans.

Moist fingers clasped the parcel containing her gold clutch, and the box containing her matching gold shoes was cradled between her arm and chest. Clara set them both on the counter then extended her arm toward the salesman behind the perfume counter. Human chatter, clicking heels, dinging registers, and the scent of colognes swirled around Clara, creating the nuisance of a headache. Joske's Department Store was a hubbub of activity.

The perfume felt cool as the attendant dabbed her wrist. She raised her arm and inhaled the scent. Clean. Not too much for a young, rural woman who felt as though she'd been dropped into a Redbook Magazine ad. A hint of homesickness elbowed her. She and Aunt Lena made fusses over the articles and advertisements each time they thumbed through the latest edition. Clara swallowed against her discomfort. She stood in a scene of surplus while images of survival paraded through her mind. Papa's income had insulated her from both extremes.

"Clara?" Hearing her name drew her attention. "Let's go wait near the door and watch for Andrew while Mother pays for the perfume."

"Mary, I am grateful, but your mother doesn't need to buy me anything else."

"Well, then tell her that yourself." Mary chuckled. "You know how much she loves to give to others. Let her do it."

Overwhelmed by the abundant Forder generosity and relieved to get away from the mixture of scents, Clara didn't hesitate to move toward the front doors with no plan to loiter in the aisles. She would stop when her feet met the sidewalk. Both her body and emotions needed to catch their breath, so the thought of fresh air appealed to her.

The moment she closed her eyes and inhaled, her emotions gasped when a familiar scent accosted them.

Wallace?

Affection warmed her.

"Clara?"

The voice lacked the deep timber that had become the sound of comfort to her. Clara opened her eyes. Andrew stood before her with his slender build. My goodness, did the man bathe in Aqua Velva? Her eyes met his staring at her from behind his rimmed glasses. A coy smile formed on his lips. He'd not offered that look before. Her pulse increased. Did he imagine kissing her?

Curiosity shamed her.

"Andrew."

Their attention changed when Mary pointed to a package Andrew held.

"You've been shopping too?"

"Yes. I bought a camera."

"A camera. May we see it?"

Andrew answered by opening the package and pulling out the black object. Clara felt a smile spread across her face. The object intrigued her. Mary touched the camera.

"It's nice, Andrew. I think it's like Garrett's camera."

"Might be. It's the latest model." He stepped back then opened the flat device revealing an extended lens. "I thought I might capture your time in San Antonio, ladies." With that, he adjusted the lens and aimed the camera toward them. Mary's hand slipped through Clara's, the parcels bumping against Clara's hip. Tilting her russet bob sideways, Clara laughed out loud, just as Andrew's finger pushed a button on the camera.

"Beautiful. Your trip to Joske's captured in time."

Clara glanced up. Indeed, bold letters portrayed its name above her.

While the Rain Whispered

Clara lay in bed next to Mary, finding it odd not to feel hair pressed between her shoulders and the pillow. Mrs. Forder, and of course Andrew, had parted ways after dinner. By the time Clara had returned from the bathroom and slipped under the covers, her friend had drifted to sleep. Clara sighed. Despite the travel from Austin, the shopping, and the sight-seeing that wearied her body, she was restless. Hadn't it been just a week when she'd lain awake at home, wrestling her thoughts over Wallace? Tonight, Andrew occupied her thoughts. His attraction unsettled her. She couldn't fool herself in to thinking the feeling didn't exist nor that it was mutual. Honor came from not giving in to the attraction.

Mary stirred. "Aren't our evening gowns lovely?" A welcome diversion.

"Beautiful."

"The Alamo is much smaller than I expected."

"Me too." Had she even wondered about its size before?

"I can't wait to see the photographs Andrew took. Imagine you and me forever in front of the Alamo."

"And Joske's, and Frosts, and along the river, and at Schilo's Restaurant with our milkshakes. You are giving me quite the adventure."

"And don't forget how we hurried back to the beauty shop for a photograph and you laughed so hard you started hiccupping."

"Ugh! The hiccup curse. It comes from Momma's side."

"I think Andrew finds you fascinating."

"I think he finds me amusing. I reckon I'm the most backwards girl he's ever met."

"You're not backwards, Clara. I reckon," Mary winked, "you're also not aware of your own charm. Goodnight. We have an early start tomorrow."

Perhaps she wasn't aware and perhaps Andrew was. Perhaps her charms were all he saw. Wallace knew both her charms and her unpleasantries, and loved her with that knowledge.

"Goodnight, Mary."

Clara returned her thoughts to Wallace. She wanted to write him again, but what would she say? I miss you. I thought of kissing Andrew? Andrew guided me up the stairs, and I liked the feel of his hand? Andrew. Andrew.

Andrew. Oh, and I cut my hair. You'd hardly recognize the woman you proposed to.

She'd write him when she was back in Austin, with some distance from the emotions hovering in San Antonio.

Clara glanced at her Bible on the nightstand. "Dear God, when I don't understand myself, I know that you still do. Help me think straight. And give sweet rest to all those I love at home."

The air felt muggy. Clara rose from the bed to adjust the window. Motion caught her eye. "Andrew?" She looked again. There was no mistaking his thin frame and the glasses. His figure dashed along the sidewalk and made a turn. Wasn't that the direction of the nightclub she'd overheard conversation about at lunch?

Nothing good could come of this late hour. Andrew, what are you up to?

Once again she was intrigued by Andrew Slayton, but this time the notion formed a knot in her stomach.

Chapter 13

Wallace couldn't argue that business was slow. With the shop closed on Mondays and the three-vehicle accident on Route Twenty, eight miles out, last Saturday, the garage was busy today. Wallace took pride in the fact that Myers Garage had the best reputation for repairs in the county. Though the business didn't bear his name, every service rendered reflected his management and skills. He rubbed the back of his neck with one hand and pushed open the screen to the Justice Store with the other. If the overhead bell announced his arrival, he didn't hear it. So often had he walked through these doors that familiarity had silenced the jingle.

"Afternoon, Maggie." Wallace glanced at Clara's friend attending the store in Henry's absence and smiled as he made his way to the post office wing of the establishment. His stride prevented any chance of conversation, forcing her soft hello to drift behind him. His intent was to open the post box.

He longed for a letter postmarked Austin, Texas to be tucked inside, awaiting his welcome. Clara had been gone eight days. He had no doubt a letter could travel from there to here in half that amount of time, giving her four days to write one. He had to admit he'd wanted to chase after the postman yesterday and dig through his mailbag when he'd found his box empty. Attending the store yesterday in place of Maggie, Wallace had jumped over the front counter and hoofed it to his box before the screen door had slammed shut behind the postman. Clara's Momma had been working the store's accounting books that day, and she too, had been disappointed to receive no letter.

Wallace unlocked the box, his thick fingers fumbling over one another. The door creaked as though yawning after a deep sleep, then opened to reveal its contents. "That's my girl!" Wallace slid his hand inside and removed the letter nestled between an auto magazine and a bill of some sort. The envelope bore his name in familiar handwriting and hailed from Austin, Texas. He slammed the door shut and lifted the letter to his nose.

No hint of Clara on the outside. No matter.

He made his way to one of the small tables near the soda fountain in front of the diner and slid his pointer finger beneath the seal, forcing himself to not tear the envelope. He didn't want to alter one piece of what Clara had touched.

Dear Wallace,

Yours is the first letter I am writing. It is Wednesday afternoon. My how time has flown. I started to write last night, Tuesday, after we arrived, but I was too tired. Our ride here was very long, made longer because Garrett stopped several times for refreshment. I was glad he did. Mary and I giggled like school girls most of the time. You would have thought us dingy. We spent the night in Waco, then got to Austin yesterday at lunch time. I can see the top of the Capitol building from the Forder's front yard. Garrett said we will go inside it while we are here.

Wallace soaked in the details of the other sights Clara described to him. Though he longed to know if she missed him, he was happy to hear her voice through written words. The aged waitress sat a glass on the table. "Your usual. A sweet tea with ice." Wallace didn't recall ordering anything, but the liquid felt good on his throat as he chugged it. He hoped he'd mumbled a thank you to the waitress, who was more wrinkled than the crumpled paper napkins left by departing customers.

You won't believe what is sitting on my night stand. My lightning bug story, typed on fancy white paper and tied with Aunt Lena's drawings in a new leather binder. I wish you could see it.

Wallace read on, counting the times the name Andrew, the son of a professor, appeared in the letter. Clara was on a first name basis with the male tutor. Nary a mention of a Mrs. Andrew Slayton. Wallace despised himself for not tamping down his jealousy. The woman he loved was joyful over her work being made presentable for whenever she met the publisher, and all he felt was hurt that someone else had done for her what he couldn't. Coupled with his shame was disappointment that after his botched proposal, he'd never gotten to hear her latest story.

He sighed. How could the same heart pray that her plans would succeed and her desires be fulfilled, yet balk at how God arranged it to happen.

He felt ill. What if her desires changed and he was no longer a part of them? Sure, she may have had good intentions by begging another proposal from him, but was the intention strong enough to counter whatever was before her in Austin?

Or whoever.

He feared her wish for another proposal was birthed by guilt over refusing him or clinging to a familiar relationship most assumed was her fate.

Next Tuesday night I will be attending a birthday party for the governor! Can you believe it? I feel like Cinderella just thinking about it.

That's tonight. Clara Williams attending the governor's birthday. Wallace rubbed his fledgling beard. She was Cinderella, except folks at home deeply loved her.

Mrs. Forder is taking Mary and me shopping Friday, promising to buy us evening dresses. Wallace, we are driving to San Antonio to shop and spend the night there. What an adventure.

His chest ached, the longing to see her was so intense.

The party is at a hotel called the Driskell. Mary says it's big and beautiful. And there are rumors it is haunted. Its walls must be filled with stories. Garrett said the publisher will be there since he is also a senator. Wallace, I hope the clock doesn't strike midnight for your Layton girl and her hopes run out the door.

My Layton girl. His lips parted in a grin.

Being sad and excited at the same time is strange, but that is how I've felt ever since Mary invited me to come here. Can you understand that?

Wallace grunted. He understood sad and worried.

How he wished he felt more excited for Clara, but the truth was, he feared he'd lose her to everything she'd ever dreamed of over everything she'd ever known. Shame invaded him. Clara was not a shallow, silly young woman and deserved more credit than he gave her. If he lost her, it wouldn't be to a whim. Loss would come because she didn't love him or she truly fell in love with another man.

I do wish you would have kissed me good-bye. But since you didn't, I am forced to imagine it, and now you are forced to imagine what I imagine.

Wallace didn't contain his laughter. Oh, Clara, if you knew what I imagine.

I will write again soon. If you see Maggie, tell her me and Mary miss her. Write me. The address is on the envelope. I hope you didn't tear it.

Yours, truly,
Clara

Wallace folded the letter and returned it to the envelope then pushed back his chair. No, he hadn't torn the address. The ending of her letter left him feeling hopeful. He'd dwell on that rather than the middle filled with accolades for Andrew Slayton. Making his way through the aisles, he grabbed a bar bath soap and reached for shaving soap, ready to give up the beard he'd nursed since Clara's departure. Just as quickly, he pulled back his hand. On second thought, he'd prefer to keep hiding behind it.

Wallace placed the soap on the counter and pulled money from his pocket.

"Need anything else, Wallace?"

He glanced behind the counter at the face belonging to the voice. Maggie Carlson was as pale as the lace collar on her dress.

"No, this is all. Maggie, are you sick?"

Her lips quivered. "I'm certain I have a fever."

"Call your parents to drive you home. I'll close up the store."

Tears rolled down her blotched cheeks. "Mama and Daddy are in Dallas seeing the doctor. So, our auto is with them. They're due in right after the store closes and will get me."

Wallace glanced at his watch. Three more hours.

"I could drive you home, if you wouldn't mind. Then come back and close up the store this evening."

"I'll be fine. But thank you."

She placed his soap into a small paper bag and shoved it toward him. Rather than taking it, he lifted a hand to her forehead.

"Maggie, you are not fine."

He turned and walked half-way toward the soda fountain before calling out to the diner cashier. "Maggie is sick. I'm taking her home, then will be back to run the store. Twenty-minutes is all I need. Can you tell any customers?" At present, the store was empty. At best, he might lose a sale or two.

"Well, I ain't allowed to ring up folks on the store register." Her words must have fought hard to push through her scowl. Wallace lassoed his frustration. "I know, ma'am. Just apologize to customers. They can wait if they want to." She shrugged her shoulders, then nodded her agreement.

Detouring to the cola machine, he paid for a Dr. Pepper, then handed it to Maggie when he reached the counter. "Drink this to cool down. Hand me the register key." She took the bottle with one hand and used her other to pull the key from her pocket. When he'd locked the cash register, he turned to see her waiting with coat and bag in hand. He thought for certain he'd seen her sway.

Grabbing her elbow, he nudged her forward. A petite hand slid around to grip his arm. "I'm awful dizzy." He paused to steady her, then led them both to his auto. The wind was heavy against them, and her grip tightened until he had her seated.

Wallace cranked the auto and drove one-handed, as was his habit. Poor girl. Maggie had been working extra shifts in Henry's absence. No doubt, from the way Clara had talked, Maggie ran the household while her mother, Amy, tended to her father.

A warm palm settled on his hand. Startled, he glanced at her. Maggie was staring at him. Words from Clara forced themselves from his memory. "Maggie is sweet on you, Wallace." He'd never taken the thought seriously. And he wasn't certain the palm of a woman in distress was validation. It was likely appreciation. "Thank you for going to this trouble. Did I see you reading a letter? From Clara?"

She removed her hand and covered her cough.

"You're welcome, and yes. Clara says she and Mary miss you. Sounds like she's having fun."

"I couldn't leave Mama and Daddy right now. Besides, the interim preacher is comin' next week from Fredericksburg, and is livin' in our back room. We had a lot to prepare. So, I turned down the trip."

"What do you know about him?"

"Nothing. I suppose Daddy knows whatever he needs to." She slumped against the door. "Tell me about Austin."

For five minutes before pulling into the parsonage gravel drive, Wallace relayed certain parts of Clara's letter, making a point not to say the name Andrew or mention daydreams of kissing.

Wallace opened the passenger door and extended his arm to Maggie. "You're too weak to walk by yourself." With the patient leaning on his arm, Wallace turned the front door knob to no avail. Maggie mumbled. "Oh, goodness. I forgot the door would be locked." Wallace banged against the wood with a fist, but heard no footsteps from inside. "Don't knock. No one's home. My brothers and sisters are staying the night at friends."

Wallace felt the shoulder against him begin to shake. "Mary, do you have a key in your bag or pocket?" The head leaning on his upper arm shook out a no. "My brother, who was the last to leave, took the spare." Wallace blew out a breath. He needed to think. Maggie needed to lie down. Right now, his strength seemed to be the reason she could remain upright.

"I'll take you to Ben and Katherine." Please God, let them be home.

While the Rain Whispered

Before Wallace could get them back to the Plymouth, Maggie doubled over and spewed the contents of her stomach. Compassion for her rushed through him. One hand held her steady while the other pulled back her hair. He eyed her as she stood upright. Maggie wiped her chin before facing him. "I'm sorry."

"I'm sorry you're sick." Again, he watched her sway, and this time, he scooped her into his arms, hoping her soiled clothing didn't press against the letter in his pocket. He'd need to change before returning to the store. Perhaps the grumpy waitress wasn't time conscious enough to hold him to his twenty minutes.

Driver and passenger made their way to the Williams home where Wallace left Maggie in the car as he bounded the steps. His knock demanded haste, and Ben responded with it.

Wallace returned to the auto and lifted Maggie in his arms. Her own encircled his neck while her head drooped against his chest where Clara's letter lay nestled in his pocket. Katherine met him at the door and indicated the front bedroom with a nod, declaring she'd return with cloths and a fresh gown. Relieved, he took the cue to leave.

As he bent to lay Maggie on the bed, her clammy hand rested above his whiskers. She slurred her words. "I like your beard. If I weren't sick, I'd kiss you. Consider yourself kissed."

For the second time in less than an hour he surmised Maggie's intentions. A kiss was validation of attraction, not appreciation. Wallace couldn't flee fast enough. His soiled shirt irritated him. He pressed against his pocket, relieved to find that spot dry. He'd had enough of Maggie. In fact, returning to the place he last saw Clara, he'd had enough of this house too. Maggie's closeness in Clara's home felt twisted.

And at some place called the Driskell, another man was probably admiring Clara in an evening dress, maybe holding her close in a dance.

His head hurt. He needed to rest it against a pillow and imagine kissing Clara, an evening gown draping the curves pressed against him.

Chapter 14
September 1937 | Austin, Texas

Clara bit her lip to stifle a gasp. The Driskell Hotel was beautiful. Relief surged through her as she felt Mary clasp her fingers and squeeze. Clara welcomed her friend's calming presence.

"What do you think?"

"I've never seen anything like it, Mary."

The elegance of her friend also stunned Clara. The pale blue satin gown, though flared at the bottom, drew attention to Mary's cobalt eyes and dark hair. Mary Forder moved with grace and complimented the surrounding sophistication. She could amble back and forth between the elite and the common, giving no hint of their distinctions. Clara admired her friend.

Running a hand over her cropped haircut, Clara pushed a loose russet curl from her eyebrow. Feeling very much like a rural girl, she fought the urge to disappear behind one of the large white pillars lining the lobby entrance. Her face warmed.

The nation's hope to recover from The Depression was still in its infancy with the New Deal. Had loss and despair even nodded to those mingling here? She chided herself, knowing the Forder businesses felt the economic pressure. Yet each survived, and her family reaped the benefit. Indeed, her family had fared much better than school mates whose families had left Layton in search of employment. The Depression had nicked Clara, but it hadn't cut her. She'd felt the adjustments Papa and Mama made in their day to day life, but life as she'd known it hadn't been abandoned.

A sparkling silver gown caught her attention. Cass Forder touched her arm with a gloved hand.

"Clara, don't be nervous. You will be just fine." Cass offered a smile. "So much for the eye to take in."

"Yes, and the heart too."

"Each attendee paid a fee to cover the food, which is being purchased at local markets and establishments and a donation to the Governor's charity of choice was required. The entry fees are paying the cooks and employees. That's good to know, isn't it?"

"Yes. Thank you."

Clara realized the burden of her own entry and donation had been paid by the Forders. Cass moved to her husband.

Clara glided her hand over the green empire gown that greeted the floor with a wide, rippling edge. Clara had been taken aback at her own reflection in their bedroom. Mrs. Forder had chosen a color that made Clara's face glow. A silk flower pin adorned the scooping neckline in colors that complimented her russet curls. Enjoy yourself, Clara.

"Ladies, follow me." Garrett kissed Cass on the cheek and tucked her arm in his. Clara and Mary fell behind Mrs. Forder and followed the senator through sitting areas and smaller lobbies, past a dining room, and to closed ballroom double doors. Music drifted into the hall. An attendant, dressed in a black tuxedo, stood at each door.

"Evening, Senator and Mrs. Forder." Chandeliers glistened overhead as Clara watched Garrett pull an invitation from his tuxedo pocket and hand it to the attendant. "Evening." The attendant glanced at the invitation, then turned his face toward Clara and the Forder women. "And welcome, Mrs. Forder, Miss Forder, and Miss Williams." He returned the invitation to Garrett, then eased the door open revealing the ballroom. "Enjoy the Governor's Birthday Ball."

Once again, Clara composed herself as she took in the scene. The ballroom was larger than her house and Aunt Lena's combined. Indeed, it must have run the length of the hotel. Clara blinked at the myriad of colors swirling in the center of the room as couples danced. Both ends of the room hosted tables decked in blue cloth, white china, red napkins, and center pieces of red and yellow roses, bluebonnets, and a small Texas state flag. A row of equally decked tables was centered on the far wall below a painted banner that read Happy Birthday Governor. A five-tiered cake was displayed in the left corner of the room. An orchestra of brass and string sat nestled against the wall on the entry side. Behind the guest seating on each end were tables laden with food arranged to appeal to the eye before appealing to the stomach. Overhead, more chandeliers twinkled, making the large space elegant, yet inviting.

Clara inhaled as childhood memories whisked through her mind. She and Aunt Lena spending hours reading fairy tales. Mary, Maggie, and her imagining themselves as princesses more times than she could recall. Momma playing records while Papa danced with his little butterfly. Wallace reminding her that she'd been kissed by angel, so she was more special than royalty.

Goodness! Here I stand, living out my imaginations—and feeling intimidated like a nervous misfit, despite Mrs. Forder's accomplishment to make my appearance as elegant as any other woman in the room. Lightheadedness threatened to create a scene. Clara shifted her feet.

Garrett's leading them toward a table was met with interruptions and introductions. Following Mary's lead, Clara smiled, offered her hand, and chatted as she deemed proper, fighting against the hiccups taunting her throat. *If only she didn't have to speak.* Just as the senator from Galveston district dismissed himself, Garrett stepped away then led a man toward them.

His build was slight, rising a mere inch above Mary. A caramel colored moustache rested above straight teeth and dimpled chin. His wide smile made him appear approachable. Clara surmised he must be an asset in social settings.

"Mrs. Forder, how good to see you again." A pleasant, deep voice.

"Please, call me Cass. Good to see you too."

Garrett placed a hand on the man's shoulder. "Ladies, meet Senator Porter Franklin."

Garrett didn't pause as he indicated each of them. "Senator, my mother, Abigail Forder. My sister Mary Forder, and her friend, Clara Williams. All here from Layton."

Porter Franklin bowed. Clara couldn't stifle her giggle and neither could Mary, thankfully. Mrs. Forder extended her hand.

"I'm honored to meet you, Ma'am. And I offer my condolences. I had the privilege of dining with your husband a couple of times when he was in Austin. A superb businessman."

"Thank you."

Clara observed Mary extend her arm as well. "It's a pleasure to meet you, Senator." Her friend blushed when the senator grasped her hand.

"The pleasure is mine, Miss Forder." Clara may not be a society girl, but she was not ignorant to the fact that the senator's eyes lit up when he spoke to Mary. She noted that Mary blushed before pulling away her hand.

Clara extended her hand to Porter Franklin. "Very nice to meet you, Senator."

"Likewise, Miss Williams. I hope you enjoy my fine city."

Garrett's laugh prevented Clara from responding. "What Porter means is that he's the Senator from this district. He grew up in Austin and never lived anywhere else. In fact, he is no stranger to politics, following in his father's footsteps." Garrett patted the man's shoulder. "Porter is a pup senator, meaning he's the youngest in either House." The man blushed as his chuckle joined Garrett's. "He started out as an aid."

The comradery between the senators amused Clara. "Garrett enjoys bringing up my days as an aid because he wants to embarrass me." He lowered his voice to a whisper. "The man is a scoundrel in my opinion."

Cass laughed. "You best watch what you say in a room full of politicians."

"Maybe you should explain yourself to these three ladies. Or perhaps you'd prefer I do the explaining." Garrett winked in the direction of the Layton ladies.

Porter smiled. "Well, ladies, you may know that a lot of teasing and bickering goes on between the two Houses. And unsuspecting aids can often find themselves caught in the middle of a joke. Most aids are young and a bit naive when they serve, much like I was. Of course, growing up with a politician, I should have known better." He cleared his throat. "Seems your honorable Garrett Forder sent me up for a prank that had me standing before the Speaker of the House with a longhorn in tow."

Mrs. Forder began to chuckle. Porter looked her way. "Exactly, Mrs. Forder, I made a complete fool of myself. The chamber erupted in laughter, stood to applaud, and broke out singing 'The Eyes of Texas Are Upon You.' My own father, sitting in the room, was in on the trick."

Laughter rang out, then at its pause, Garrett spoke.

"Aside from being a politician, Porter is a publisher." The room spun. Clara's skin became clammy. "His family runs Porterhouse Publishing." She felt Mary brush her arm. "Porter, Clara is the author I spoke with you about."

Doubts converged on her reasoning. Clara flashed back to her room at home and the hours bent over a tablet with a pencil in hand, scribbling out words before they turned and ran. Stacks of writing tablets in her room. Her audience comprised of loved ones. So safe. So simple. So crude. So unprofessional. Any dignity her stories carried came from Aunt Lena's drawings. No matter how Andrew had packaged her work, its value came from the love of family and friends. Why had she allowed the situation to come to this? She'd turned down a marriage proposal to find herself standing here, a raw and unrefined writer. Like the setting where she stood, Porter Franklin and his publishing house were for the elite writers destined to fill bookstores and libraries. She should have remained content in her simplicity. The Forder graciousness exceeded her talent.

Clara wanted to look at the ground, but made herself face the senator.

"I suspected such." He smiled, then directed his attention to her. "Miss Williams, I think highly of Garrett and his opinion. So, I have taken liberty to set an appointment with you for next week. Provided I am able to leave the session. Garrett can inform you of details."

Wallace had released her for this opportunity. The magnitude of his action warmed her, slowing her rapid heartbeat and settling her shallow breaths. God had brought these events together. She'd not done it herself. She pushed aside the doubts to speak.

"I'm very honored that you'd meet with me. Thank you." Had the words reached him or had she imagined speaking them?

"I look forward to it. We are looking for children's stories, so our meeting is timely. Please bring your sample manuscript with you."

At last, she allowed the magnitude of the opportunity to sink in and bounced on her toes. Excitement formed into a grin that she felt from cheek to cheek. "Yes, I will. Thank you again."

"It's my pleasure. And speaking of pleasure, Miss Forder," his gaze now locked on Mary, "once you've found your table, might I have your first dance?"

"'I'd be delighted." Her friend's eyes, wide and glowing, were dancing already.

Clara eased into the magic of the evening, sitting next to Mrs. Forder sipping punch and nibbling on shrimp dipped in a red sauce. She'd never tasted the cold, cooked delight. Her eyes roamed the ballroom. Garrett was the striking image of his father as he moved among the crowd with Cass at his side. A glance at Mary and Porter revealed smiles and lips moving in conversation. Clara expected to spot Andrew who was supposed to attend with his family. She'd not seen him since they arrived back in Austin.

She surmised by his absence at church Sunday, Andrew worshiped elsewhere. Or nowhere? With Madie still sick, he'd not been needed for tutoring. His absence brought her relief from the attraction she felt for him and returned her thoughts to Wallace where they belonged. Certainly natural curiosity was all that had her looking for Andrew now. Clara released a slight breath, wary of wavering over Andrew Slayton.

Mary and Porter returned to the table each holding a glass of punch. Just as Porter seated Mary, offering to bring her a plate, Clara no longer wondered about Andrew. His tall figure flanked by a woman and a man, ambled toward the table. Mrs. Forder spoke his name, and Porter turned to face them. "Ah, Professor & Mrs. Slayton. It's been a while. Good to see you." The elder man reflected Andrew's facial features. The woman carried his build.

The men shook hands. "Porter, this is our son, Andrew." Once again two men shook hands. Andrew's voice filled the air, introducing Mary and Mrs. Forder to his parents, explaining who they were in relation to Garrett and the student he tutored. His parents responded with comments and questions. Clara felt awkward. After all, she reckoned, she was not a noteworthy connection in need of introduction. Clara lowered her head feigning an adjustment to her napkin.

His cologne announced itself beside her. Clara raised her face, sensing Andrew standing next to her chair. He no longer donned the scent of Wallace James. The spicy aroma was distinctly his, as was the smile he gave her.

"And this is Mary's friend from home, Clara Williams."

Professor and Mrs. Slayton smiled. "It's good to meet you. Welcome to Austin."

"Thank you. I'm pleased to meet you both."

With that, Mr. Slayton excused he and his wife to the refreshments.

"Andrew, please join us."

"Perhaps I will, Mary, once Clara and I have danced."

Her cheeks heated.

"That is, if Miss Williams would do me the honor."

She was here. She was dressed for a ball, and Andrew stood in a tux offering his arm, something Wallace would do were he present.

He was not.

"I'd love to dance, Andrew."

She stepped into the role of Cinderella.

His movements were smooth as they glided across the dance floor keeping pace with the lively tune. Did he think her a bulky dancer? As the orchestra transitioned to a slow selection, she felt his hand move from her shoulder and clasp her waist. He pulled her closer, then lowered his head to her ear. The rim of his glasses grazed her temple. "You're beautiful, Clara." Her skin tingled. "I've missed you." He tucked her head against his shoulder.

My goodness.

She was at ease in his arms. The realization surprised her.

"You don't know me enough to miss me, Andrew."

"I know what I've observed. I know what I've looked upon."

His hand brushed her cheek.

Clara Williams felt far from Layton, and the feeling had nothing to do with distance.

Romance suffocated reason.

Chapter 15

SEPTEMBER 1937 | LAYTON, TEXAS

"Your friend." That's how he'd decided to sign the letter he wrote to Clara last night. Wallace ran the sentiment through his mind. He'd wanted to end expressing his love, but he couldn't bring himself to do it. He'd bid Clara off free as butterfly, and didn't regret that decision. He had not written a love letter. Diplomacy defeated desire.

The truth was he had little to write because there was so much to be said that must remain unsaid. There was no mention of his weekend sulking at Ma's, of Maggie's closeness, of Henry's dark spell, his beard, his loneliness, or his love.

> *Maggie was sick when I saw her at the store last night. With her family gone, I took her to your parents. She told me that the interim preacher is arriving next week. He's coming from Fredericksburg, which is not too far from Austin.*
>
> *The garage has been busy, sadly because of a wreck over the weekend.*
>
> *By the time you read this, the governor's party will be past. I sure hope you enjoyed yourself. I have no doubt you were the most beautiful young lady there. Surely the only one kissed by an angel. I hope you got to meet the publisher. Clara, I don't doubt one bit that he (or she) will want to print your stories.*

On and on the letter had run mentioning mundane matters she could compare to Austin adventures. Perhaps he shouldn't mail it. Keeping her curious could be in his favor.

He walked the three hundred feet from his garage to the Justice Store to mail the letter.

"Mornin' Katherine, can I bring you some coffee?" Wallace smiled at Clara's mother.

"No, thanks, got some already."

"Heard any more about Maggie?"

91

"She's still sick. I'm running the store again today."

"I reckoned so. I can relieve you after the garage closes."

"Thanks, but I'll be fine. Lena is cooking supper for us at her house. You should join us."

His chest tightened at the thought.

"Well, alright. Thank you. Sure Lena won't mind?"

He smiled as Katherine laughed aloud.

"Right. Of course she won't." It would be good to see for himself how Henry fared.

"Heard from Clara?"

"No. Have you?"

"Yes." Heat rose beneath his beard.

Her eyes grew big and she smiled. He sensed her relief or was it hope?

"Well, any news—that you can share?"

"Plenty." And the tutor remained nameless in the retelling.

He mailed his letter and began trotting back to the garage when he spotted a black Ford parked outside it. He knew full well who owned the automobile. Wallace slowed his pace. Walter Myers had every right at any time to visit the garage he owned. However, he rarely did, at least unannounced. It had been nine months since Wallace had traveled to Galveston for them to meet in person. Walter owned a larger auto garage in that city and had called it home for the past six years. In the scheme of things, Wallace figured the Layton garage was nothing much to Walter, although it was everything to him.

Wallace pushed open the office door. Dressed in a black suit, Walter stood with his back to him, reading the label on a can of motor oil. He turned when the door hinges squeaked.

"Walter."

"How you doing, Wallace?"

"Fairly well. Good, in fact."

Walter placed the can on the shelf. "That brand is a good seller."

"Sure is. Want some coffee?"

"No, thanks. You've grown a beard."

"Just recently."

"The garage looks good. I introduced myself to the new mechanic."

"He's a good guy. Does good work." He'd not mention his habit of arriving late. "Yeah, things are going good."

With the garage.

Silence settled in. Wallace cleared his throat. "You here to see the books?" Walter raised the right side of his lip. Wallace noted the sweat on his brow. "No, I'm here for another reason." Walter dusted the metal chair in the office corner and sat down. Wallace followed suit and pulled out the desk chair. "Wallace, I'll get right down to business. The garage has to be shut down."

He glared.

"Why?"

"The garage in Galveston is shut down already. I accumulated debt trying to keep it open when business slowed. I borrowed against this garage to save the other and also used most of my own money. Now this loan is coming due and the profit isn't enough to pay off the loan."

Wallace worked to temper his anger. "Myers is the best garage this side of the county. It's struggled, but survived the lean years because of that reason. You jeopardized it." Not to mention my livelihood. Wallace rose and stood in front of the man.

"It's business, Wallace, in hard times. Don't take it personally."

"Walter, it's gonna feel personal—to a lot of folks."

Walter's face turned red. "Don't you think I know that, Wallace? The good Lord knows I'm losing every penny. It's my family that's jeopardized."

Wallace relented and shook his head in understanding.

"Look, Wallace. This garage is successful because of you. I'm not ignorant to that fact. Nor do I want to cut off your livelihood."

"Well, it seems that's about to happen."

"Hear me out. I tried to sell it." The words slapped Wallace. "But no investor is interested in a small garage in and of itself. And its location in the so-called Forder Empire makes hopes for expanding property futile for an investor. It's just not a good business deal. Even if I'd sold it, that wouldn't guarantee you work."

Wallace blew out a breath. "Seems we're doomed."

"I want to offer you the shop. If you can afford to pay off the loan against this shop, it's yours. I'll sign it over to you free and clear. Otherwise the bank takes over and shuts it down."

Wallace rubbed his forehead.

"Walter, I don't have that amount of money."

"You don't even know the amount."

"No need to know, especially if the profits can't cover it."

Walter stood. "Look, you got until the end of the month to decide before the loan is called in and we shut down. Think about it. Talk to a banker if you need to. I'll be in touch again." Walter extended his hand. Wallace took it, feeling as though he shook on the end of everything he'd had to offer Clara. "The price and details are written down here." Walter tapped a folded piece of paper on the desk as he walked out.

Wallace tromped into his private room and slammed the door behind him. He'd never been a cursing man and didn't grow up around it, yet such words now filled his mind unbidden. He was certain he'd never felt this angry. When Clara had turned down his proposal, he'd felt devastation, but not anger. He shook the baffling reaction and dropped to his knees at the bed. "God, please don't take my livelihood away. Why would you bring me through such lean years, build up business, then snatch it from me? First Clara, now the garage. Are my hopes and dreams a joke to you?" He became aware of the tears rolling down his cheeks. "God, truth is, I know I can trust you, so I will, but I'm gonna need your help to do it."

The box springs squeaked as he pressed against the bed and rose to his full height. He headed back to the desk. His impulse to telephone Ben went unchecked. He asked the switchboard operator to ring the Forder offices. The need to share his burden with flesh and blood was stifling, and his Pa had no telephone. After two rings a female voice responded.

"Celeste, this is Wallace James. Could Ben come to the telephone?" Celeste and her husband had been rescued from the cotton fields by Mason Forder and put to work in his businesses. Wallace had a fondness for them because Celeste had helped Katherine birth Clara into the world.

"Hello, Wallace. Good to hear your voice. You hold on while I check."

When Ben answered, Wallace felt his muscles twitch. He realized Ben might respond less as a friend and more like the father of the woman to whom Wallace had offered provision.

"Wallace?"

"Walter is losing the garage."

Silence. Wallace wiped his clammy palm on his pants leg.

"Why?"

"He borrowed against it to keep the Galveston shop afloat, but it didn't recover. He's going bankrupt."

"When?"

"A month. He says if I pay off the loan, the garage is mine free and clear. I've got until the end of the month before the loan is called in."

"He doesn't want to sell it instead of lose it?"

Wallace explained.

Ben cleared his throat. "So you've got a little time to figure things out."

By saying "things" was he including Clara—if she still wanted him. Wallace rubbed his forehead.

"Yes, I reckon I do, but facts are facts. I can't pay off the loan."

'How much?"

"He wrote it down, but I didn't look because I know what I got set aside. Said the profits aren't enough to pay it. Look, Ben, like I said, facts are facts."

"Not everything is left to fact. Some things ought to be left to faith."

At the moment his faith felt stretched as thin as his finances.

"I'm a man of faith, but not an ignorant one."

"I never said you were."

"Clara. I got to provide for Clara—if she would still want me."

"I know. I got to hang up. We'll talk more, Wallace. But not tonight in front of Henry. I reckon you got invited."

"I did. And of course. Thanks, Ben."

The lines disconnected. Wallace turned around and noted an immediate concern. His mechanic stood in the open doorway between the office and work area. How much had he overheard?

"So, you gonna buy this place?"

The simple answer was no, but there was nothing simple about answering.

Wallace slid fingers up and down the beard where clean shaven skin should have been. The whiskers felt misplaced. Like him. He stood on Henry and Lena's front porch. "I don't belong here." The night air listened. He came tonight with his mind deflated by Walter Myer's news. Although Ben hadn't been discouraging, that conversation also pestered him. He couldn't put a finger on how Ben had felt. Maggie was another dilemma nagging at him. Hindsight heightened her hints of romance.

Adding to the weight he carried, memories of the last gathering with these families seized his appetite. Feigned images of Clara seated next to a husband from Austin mocked him. These folks may not be his people for much longer. Were it not for the need to assuage his fears of how Henry was faring, Wallace would be just about any place but here with people he loved.

He remembered Lena and Henry's child dying. He even remembered that Henry had hidden himself away for months while he grieved. He knew the family dubbed the period Henry's darkness. What Wallace didn't recall was despair ebbing from Henry's being as it did this moment. Perhaps he'd been on the fringe of becoming close enough knit with the family to sense Henry's agony.

The atmosphere in the usually cheerful home felt heavy with gloom, and Wallace fought to not give into the aura, heightened by the tug of emotions from his past few days. The two families around whom Clara's life revolved were a tight fit in the living room. The home was warm with kitchen heat, and the aroma of fried chicken pushed its way through the thick gloom.

Wallace chuckled listening to the children's attempts to outdo one another's school stories. To overhear them, he could think the youngsters oblivious to Henry's condition, but he'd noticed their glances toward the man. Perhaps they hoped the stories made him smile or perhaps they hoped their voices didn't agitate him. He turned his attention back to the adults. Lena, whom Wallace had never known to sit still for long, sat next to Henry on the couch. Henry's food appeared untouched although he seemed to study the chicken leg on his plate.

"Lena, this chicken tastes real good."

"Thank you, Wallace."

"I might have to steal Henry's pieces from him."

"You can have 'em." Wallace felt his eyes bulge as Henry held up a leg and thigh. "I told you, Lena, that I didn't want dark meat. Do I need to tell you a hundred times before you remember?"

Wallace's stomach sank. He watched Lena purse her lips. The sarcasm and tone mocked the genuine Henry. Knowing Henry wasn't his amiable self, Wallace had weighed his teasing before speaking, but the harm had been unpredictable.

"Henry, I must not have heard you right when we were in the kitchen. I thought you pointed to those two pieces on the platter and said you wanted them."

"Well, you didn't tell me they were dark."

Wallace wanted to defend Lena. They'd begun to love one another while cooking at a boarding house. The man certainly knew which pieces of chicken were white and which were dark.

"Here, take my white piece instead. You know I'm rather fond of the dark meat."

Lena gave her husband a wink as she traded the pieces. Henry bit into the chicken breast without a thank you. Lena smiled. Wallace relaxed. He reckoned Lena didn't need defending. She needed support. Henry needed understanding. Though the picture wasn't pretty, it was priceless. Wallace knew he was gazing on love and commitment.

Supper wound down and Wallace found himself alone in the living room with the women. He apologized for the uproar he'd started.

Lena smiled at him. "Wallace, I was relieved to hear some anger."

"Relieved?" He rubbed his forehead.

"Henry's seemed to feel nothing for days. Seeing any emotion gives me hope he's gonna be out of this soon. We'll work through this. And pray. A lot."

Katherine interjected. "Wallace, Henry asked about Clara when Ben and me got here. Maybe you should tell him the news from her letter."

"You got a letter?" Lena leaned up in her seat.

"Yessum."

A figure carrying wood pushed open the screen with his elbow and entered the room. Lena stood to her feet. "Henry, Wallace got a letter from Clara, and he's gonna tell us all about her news." A broad smile spread across the man's face giving the room a glimpse of the Henry they all knew.

Wallace's breath stalled. Clara brightened a room without even being present. *That's my girl.*

Night set in and Wallace returned home. Lying on his bed he replayed the evening then glanced at the neglected bottle of Aqua Velva sitting on the small table. His visit with Lena and Henry reminded him of two things. Despite the bad news of late, Wallace had both the faith and the capacity to work through it. And despite the cause, if he lost Clara, he'd never stop loving her.

A knock on the garage door startled him. He wrinkled his forehead. Who'd need auto service this late at night? "Coming." He knew the tone was rude and sharp. And he regretted it immediately when he opened the door to Ben.

"Reckon we ought to finish that talk."

"Now?"

"Yep. Start talking."

Wallace motioned for Ben to sit, then yanked on the light and seated himself on top of the metal desk.

"It's simple. The garage is closing. I can't buy it. I love your daughter. I can't provide for her."

"You planning on being without a job for the rest of your life?"

"Lands sake, Ben. You know I don't. But I don't know what work I'll find. I might not be able to support one person. Let alone a family."

"A man who's found his love and is supposed to be living a married life and ain't makes for a miserable man."

"A man who can't care for his love makes for a miserable man."

"Wallace. Never since I've known you have I seen you this unreasonable. You're stubborn. If Clara returns and has come to her senses about marrying you, do it. Neither of you will be complete without the other. I'm telling you, as a friend, as a man, it's misery."

Pain contorted the man's face. "Ben?"

"I'm speaking from heartbreaking experience. Thank God he untangled my mess. I'm the most content man on this earth." He leaned forward. "Talk to God, then shut your trap and listen."

Ben's intensity agitated him. Wallace smirked. "And if she doesn't want me?"

Ben Williams stood, and sighed. His eyes pooled with tears. "I reckon, Wallace, that would be the beginning of your real problem."

The men shook hands. "I came tonight as a friend, and I won't pressure you no more. I'm walking out of here a Papa. Like I said when Clara left, I love my daughter, and I'll be there for her no matter what."

Wallace shut and locked the door, yanked the light off, then undressed for bed and crawled in.

A snap coming from the trap in the office made him shudder. "That's one problem solved."

He closed his eyes and prayed that his sound mind could guide his muddled heart.

Chapter 16
SEPTEMBER 1937 | AUSTIN, TEXAS

Once again Clara pulled out the letter she'd started to Wallace two days ago then stuffed into her drawer. It was dated Wednesday, and here she sat Friday morning, a mere date and greeting its only contents. This man had invaded her being, yet she couldn't face him, not even with pen and paper.

When she and Andrew had parted at the Driskell, Clara hardly recognized herself. The girl from Layton was ashamed of the young woman in Austin whose physical sensations had reacted to Andrew's closeness. Those feelings had been stifled with Wallace, and only recently had she allowed them to emerge and take a breath around him. Here in Austin they ran reckless and had to be tended like untamed children. She found herself curious if life as Mrs. Andrew Slayton would be a perfect fit.

So, anytime she'd pulled out the letter, either her conscious taunted her or Andrew's presence tutoring Madie in the dining room distracted her.

She plopped onto her bed and placed the letter on a book she'd found on the floor. Maybe God would make sense of her prayers for help, uttered in choppy thoughts and inadequate words. "I want to do what's right."

"What'd you say?" Madie walked through the door.

"Oh. Just talking to myself." The young girl giggled. "I do that too. Don't worry, you're normal." Clara crossed her eyes and made fish lips. "You surr adoubt dat?" Madie laughed. "I got to do my math before Mr. Slayton comes, but I can't find my book."

Clara surrendered the book she'd picked up and moved to lean over the small bedside table. Madie paused before leaving. "Mr. Slayton sure does smile when he looks at you. I think he loves you." Clara's breath hitched and she felt heat rise on her cheeks. Had he said something to Madie, of all people? "Mr. Slayton does not love me. Silly girl." Madie walked out, then turned to face her. "I got eyes you know. I can see how he looks all goofy when you come in the room." Mary passed her sister coming into the room.

"I'm right, aren't I Mary?"

"About what?"

100

"Just say yes." Madie giggled and continued down the hall without explanation.

"Is that the letter to Wallace?" Mary seemed unconcerned over Madie's remark. Her friend sat down beside her. Clara shifted as the bed gave way.

"If you can call it a letter. Mary, I'm confused."

"Andrew seems smitten with you."

"First Madie, now you."

"It's obvious. But one thing Madie and me haven't caught on to is how you feel about him."

"I like being around him. I feel charmed. I feel pretty. I feel attracted. But I don't feel whole. And I feel real guilty."

"You haven't misbehaved, Clara. But maybe you've misjudged either how you feel about Wallace or how you feel about Andrew. You'll figure things out." Mary took her hand and squeezed. "And remember, Wallace turned you down so you could come here free as butterfly. Those were your exact words to me. So, if you're ever going to explore your feelings, now's the time." Mary bounced off the bed and grabbed the stationery sitting on her dresser. "You write Wallace. I'll write Maggie."

Clara reached for the pen in her drawer, but her manuscript caught her eye. Contentment spread through her as she took in the sight. Did God intend for her words and Lena's pictures to be printed for hundreds, maybe thousands to read? If Porterhouse Publishers turned it down, would the joy of the consideration fade into the pain of rejection? She hoped not.

An image came to mind of Wallace bent over the engine of Papa's auto listening to her tales as he worked. She knew he'd be happy for her if she got published, but a publishing house name wouldn't make her stories more endearing to him. A longing to see him awoke, and in that moment she put pen to paper and began to write.

...and as much fun as I'm having, I miss knowing what's happening at home. Wallace, sometimes I feel like a real city girl, then other times, I feel like I'm living in a pretend story. Stop smiling! I imagine you telling me to quit thinking too much and just enjoy myself.

He wouldn't say that if he saw me around Andrew.

Today we are going to eat lunch near the Capitol building, then Garrett is going to show us around. I might see the publisher again. He's a Senator too — the youngest one right now. His name is Porter Franklin, and his family owns Porterhouse Publishers. Keep this secret, but I think he has eyes for Mary.

Did you ever catch the mouse in your office? I sure miss Maggie. I hope Momma and Papa got my postcard. Did they show it to you?

Clara had grown familiar with Andrew's knock and greeting each morning, so when the sounds seeped under the closed doorway, she kept her composure, despite her fickle heart's attempt to flutter.

"Andrew's here. I hope he brought the photographs." Clara looked up to see Mary folding Maggie's letter while she spoke. "Me too. Let's go find out." A wide grin made itself at home, for Clara truly was excited to see the photographs. She set aside the letter and went to look in the mirror. The short hair in her reflection still took her by surprise. Madie opened the door. "Mr. Slayton brought these." She held up a small brown envelope and wiggled it in the air. "Mommy says we can all look at them at the dining room table. I don't even have to start my lessons yet." Mary walked out behind Clara and called out to her mother to join them, but Clara saw she was already in the front room. The smell of coffee and bacon still lingered in the air, mixing with Andrew's after shave.

"Morning, Andrew." Thoughts of Wallace shied away when Andrew's smile greeted her. "Morning, Clara."

The company of them sat around the table and passed the pictures from one to another. Clara laughed when she saw the picture of her outside the salon. "Look at my wide eyes. I think I was wondering what folks back home will think." What Wallace would think. She had almost forgotten about the picture of she and Mary showing off new trousers for Cass to see when they returned. "We both look so tall."

Her breath caught when Andrew passed the next photograph. She didn't know it had been taken. There she was in his arms, looking up at him as they danced. She glanced at Andrew now and knew he recognized her curiosity over who took the photograph, for he shrugged his shoulders. A roguish smile spread across his lips.

"Oh my."

The words slipped out without permission and peaked Mary's interest who reached for the image and squealed when she saw it. "Porter took this. The camera was on the table. He winked and said Andrew wouldn't mind." Clara bet he didn't. Indeed, she wondered if Andrew had conspired with Porter.

"It's a divine picture. He took one of me. Is it in there, Andrew?"

"The next one. I'd say you look like royalty, Mary." She giggled. Clara warmed at his kindness.

The last photograph was passed around the table, then Cass spoke up.

"Time for school, Madie." The child gave a courtesy groan. Andrew rose. "We want to finish before you leave for lunch and the Capitol."

"Thank you for showing us the photographs." Clara smiled at Andrew, then he handed her the envelope.

"They're yours to keep."

"Mine? Oh, thank you."

She pulled the envelope to her chest as she and Mary headed back to the room where they went through the photographs again. She considered sending one to Wallace, but hesitated when she realized he'd see her in short hair. She surmised by the way he fingered her curls that he loved her long locks, and why it mattered so much at this moment, she couldn't determine. She was relieved when Mary didn't suggest sending one to Maggie. She reckoned Mary knew the dilemma Clara faced.

The telephone rang. Within minutes, Mrs. Forder tapped on the bedroom door. "Mr. Porter Franklin is on the telephone, Mary. He's asked my permission to join us for lunch and the Capitol if you'd welcome that." Both girls jumped from their beds and hugged one another.

"What did you say?"

"I said I would welcome his company, but it was not my decision to make." Mrs. Forder kissed Mary on the forehead. "He's on the line waiting for you to answer him."

If the twinkle in her eyes and the grin on her lips were any indication, Madie had extended Andrew the invitation to join their excursion. Here he was pulling out her chair next to his around the large round dining table. Clara smiled at Madie across the table, and her eager face turned a shade of pink. Clara realized that the grin on Madie's face may also stem from the fact that Porter Franklin was seated next to Mary.

Andrew's shoulder brushed against her arm as he leaned in. His breath was warm against her cheek. "What will you order?" Her eyes were glued to the prices on the menu. Never had she paid this much for food. Of course, she wasn't paying for it now. She cleared her throat. She wanted steak. He suggested lasagna for its rich flavors and texture. Clara giggled. That is how Wallace describes his rabbit stew.

"I can't believe you kill little bunnies then cook 'em and eat 'em."

"Take a bite. It's rich with flavor and texture."

"And fur?"

"Put the spoon in your mouth, Clara."

The memory made Clara miss him.

"Lasagna is layers of cheese, thick pasta noodles, and beef in red sauce. If you don't like the taste, we will trade plates and you can eat my steak." Huh? Oh, Andrew.

"Promise?"

"I do, but trust me, you're in for an adventure."

She had collected herself enough to be back in the moment and looked him in the eyes.

"Trust you? I will. And, I like a good adventure."

His eyes widened and one side of his mouth lifted. "I'll keep that in mind." She wished she could take back her words. Had he read more into them than she intended?

The clinking of silverware and glassware amidst chatter filled the afternoon meal. Beside her Mary and Porter talked and laughed in apparent infatuation with one another. Contentment moved through Clara. She'd never seen Mary so taken by anyone. She caught Mrs. Forder looking across the table at the couple. The grin on her face hinted at approval and joy. Clara glanced at Cass who raised her eyebrows and smiled when their eyes met. The message between them clear. They both were happy for Mary.

Clara took the last bite of the lasagna. Andrew had not misled her. The pasta concoction was delicious. She'd have to figure out the recipe and share it with Aunt Lena. Sipping the last of her sweet tea, she mustered the courage to appease her curiosity over a matter.

"Andrew, I haven't seen you at the church where the Forders go."

"With good reason. I'm not there."

"So you go to another church?"

"I didn't say that."

"So you don't go to church?"

"Honestly Clara, I don't see the need for church. Does that offend you?"

Offend? She supposed "concern" was the better word.

"Well, I reckon I'm not offended. But I don't understand. Do you believe in God and Jesus?"

He chuckled "You sound like my Sunday School teacher when I was five years old."

Now she felt offended.

"I'm sorry, Clara. I embarrassed you."

"Do you believe in them?"

"Yes, and I don't need church membership to prove my belief."

She squirmed in her seat not knowing how to argue his point.

"There's something else I want to ask you."

"So we're done with the subject of church?"

"For now."

He smirked.

"Andrew, one night in San Antonio I couldn't sleep, so I was looking out the window and saw you leave the hotel. Where did you go so late at night?"

He pressed his lips together, then offered a cold smile. Her skin tightened at his look.

"You're a curious one."

"I like adventure." She bit her tongue at using the phrase again.

"Well, the telling of that night's adventure will have to wait."

He winked, and unlike the teasing winks Papa gave, Andrew's seemed threatening. She exaggerated a wink in return. "For now."

The waiter paused to her right and offered more tea. "Oh! My dress." Clara startled in her chair and felt it lean back. "Careful!" Andrew grabbed her chair. The waiter was pulling a napkin from his apron and offering it to her. Tea saturated her dress. "My sincere apology, Miss."

Clara dabbed at the stain. She'd debated between the navy and burnt orange dresses this morning. She'd made a good choice. The stain would be less evident against the navy. Andrew stood beside her, and she realized he was speaking harshly to the waiter whose face was flaming red. The entire table had noted his mistake.

"I'm fine, Andrew. Thank you." His tone was embarrassing her. She turned to the waiter.

"Our staff will make amends, Miss."

"Not necessary. Perhaps some water and towels are all I need if you could point me toward a sink."

"I'll escort you to the ladies lounge." Andrew drew back her chair and offered his hand. She would much prefer to go alone, but Andrew seemed more bothered than she. Clara reckoned a short stroll through the restaurant might settle him. She addressed her friends. "I'll be right back. Don't order that dessert Garrett talked about without me." Mary scooted back her chair. "I'm fine, Mary. You stay."

Andrew guided her through the maze of tables, then stood in the narrow hallway outside the door of the ladies' room. As she stepped back out, he glanced around before embracing her.

"Andrew. Stop worrying. My dress and me are fine."

"Yes, Clara, you are so fine that it's all I could do to not take your hand in mine at the table. You look delicious this afternoon."

Delicious? She squirmed against his tight hold, then maneuvered her head to see him. "Did you pay the waiter to do that?" She hoped to lighten the moment so he'd release her. She felt uncomfortable, perhaps ashamed, in such a public setting. And besides, both his answers and his dismissal of her questions nagged at her.

Andrew laughed, then placed a finger on her angel kiss. Her heart thudded while something in her conscience gave warning. The mark had been the source of disdain until Wallace declared he cherished it. In fact, she knew all those she loved considered her mark a beauty all her own. Had Andrew come to cherish it as well? "If you'd permit me, I'd try to kiss this mark away." Her stomach rolled. She squirmed from his embrace, sensing the suggestion was less about the fervor of his kiss and more about disfavor of her mark.

"You don't care for my angel kiss?"

"It is the one blemish on your beauty."

What? For all he knew, she was covered in blemishes he could not see. Clara thought of her Papa's burn scars from years back. Hidden to the world, but seen by those who loved him. She pushed away from Andrew but locked eyes with him. His arms dropped to his side.

"It is my one, unique beauty."

She turned toward the dining room.

"Clara, forgive me."

"We need to get back to the table."

She'd told him when they danced that he didn't know her. He hadn't denied it.

"I know what I see…"

Andrew excused himself after the lunch, offering regrets that he couldn't join them at the Capitol. He'd supposedly forgotten about a prior commitment. Despite his suspicious excuse, Clara felt relieved. She needed distance between them.

After they slid into the backseat of Garrett's car, Mary touched her arm.

"Clara, are you alright? Andrew was practically sulking the remainder of lunch."

"Everything is alright."

But it was not. Her instinct told her there was something very wrong about Andrew Slayton.

Chapter 17

SEPTEMBER 1937 / LAYTON, TEXAS

Good. Henry agreed to help. Wallace wasn't certain if Henry would show up tomorrow morning or if his condition would render him useless if he did, but he'd be happy to have his skill nearby nonetheless. Marriage or no marriage, he would fix up the house on the edge of town belonging to his second cousin. The imminent closing of the garage would render him both jobless and homeless.

His shoulders slumped at the thought of moving in alone. For more years than he could respectfully admit, he'd imagined eating and sleeping with Clara, a gaggle of youngins' at their feet. What would she think upon her return to see him fixing the house? She could think him presumptuous that she would still want to marry him. She could also think he had resigned himself to life without her. The one thing she probably wouldn't suspect is that he couldn't guarantee the provisions she deserved. Overthinking the matter made him queasy.

He regretted that he couldn't buy the house outright. With his job instability, using up his savings was too risky. Wallace was grateful Ma's cousin had agreed to rent him the house for five dollars a month.

He studied his surroundings and laughed at himself. "Feeling nostalgic." He'd been comfortable in this small side room for six years, though the only things he could call his own were the clothes, quilt, dishes, and a few personal items. And a folded piece of tablet paper with a title written on it. He'd burn it with a match before he left. He shouldn't have it in his possession.

Nostalgia gave way to guilt, but he ignored it. Over the years, he'd become good at ignoring the guilt over taking the paper, but more so over not confessing it. The child-sized act had matured into adult-sized deception.

The smell of Ma's canned soup filled the air. He slipped a heaping spoon of the warm liquid into his mouth and checked off the last item on his list. Between what Henry offered to bring and what was kept in the garage, Wallace had the tools he needed for minor repairs. At least he hoped the house repairs were minor. It had been a year since he'd seen the place. He lifted the bowl to his mouth and gulped down the last bit of soup. He had to face facts. Life was changing, and not in the way he'd imagined just a few days ago.

Perhaps he'd do that tomorrow.

He washed the bowl, set an alarm, then fell fully clothed onto his bed. Today needed to end. Morning would be here soon enough.

Gravel popped outside the garage indicating an auto had pulled up. The sun offered another day. Wallace glanced at his watch. Ma and Pa were right on time. He smiled and headed out to greet them. A glance into the backseat of the auto revealed it was laden with boxes. No doubt, Ma had been busy packing the things a man didn't realize he needed when he moved into a house. Wallace laughed.

"Morning."

Both Ma and Pa widened their eyes when they saw him.

"Morning, Wallace." Pa shook his hand and joined in the laughter, pointing his head to the backseat. "Your Ma's doin's."

"I reckoned." Her cheek was warm when he pecked it. "Thank you. My beard's gettin' bushy, ain't it?"

"Hides that handsome face God gave you." Ma patted his bearded jawline then pressed her hand over his heart. "But it don't hide the hurt in here. I reckon it draws attention to it. But since you're a grown man, I ain't got no say in such things." Her head wobbled back and forth.

Ma had a way of speaking truth to the little boy tucked inside his large frame.

She pointed toward the backseat. "I sewed you some curtains. Rummaged and got you some more pans and dishes." Wallace appreciated her kindness and regretted it at the same time. The truth rested where his heart touched his soul—nothing was right about this arrangement. Clara should be the one sewing curtains and setting dishes in the cupboard. He wrinkled his brow to ward off the despair posing as a headache. "It's to hold you over until the future Mrs. Wallace James sets up house. Have faith."

Faith? It had scurried off at the moment.

Wallace loaded his tools into the Plymouth and hopped into the driver seat and began to lead the way. Henry was meeting them at the house. Making a right turn off the main road, he maneuvered over a large pot hole and eased onto Cotton Gin Road, which resembled more of a lane speckled with weeds and ruts. When he was a boy this had been the route to Forder Gin. Like him, the town had grown, and this route had evolved into a memory. Dust flew from his tires and circled the auto behind him. Surely, with the cool air, Pa had rolled up the windows before taking off. Otherwise, Ma would be wheezing and sneezing the rest of the morning.

Four dwellings greeted the travelers as they drove the two mile stretch toward the place he would call home. They testified to wear and tear. He'd noted lopsided porches, chipped paint, a crumbled chimney, and yards overtaken by weeds. Dread passed through him. Was his house in this condition?

He pulled onto the gravel drive that was laden with weeds. He was happy to see Henry's auto parked outside and his friend walking from around back of the house. Henry waved. Wallace opened his door and stepped outside. Relief swept through him although he stood in knee deep weeds and grass. From first sight, aside from a screen door dangling on the front porch, the outside structure of his house appeared in tact just as it had a year ago when he and Pa had come by to tend it.

"Morning, Henry. How's it looking?" Along with being a skilled cook, Henry had a natural gift for repair and renovation.

"Got some boards to replace on the back porch. One of the windows is cracked. The shed is leaning. 'Course I hadn't been inside. Looks good considering you hadn't tended to it. "

"He hadn't, but I have from time to time." Pa walked up and shook Henry's hand while Wallace stared at him.

"Pa, you been here since we last came?"

"Yep, about four or five times."

"When?"

"It don't matter."

Wallace glanced at Henry, who shrugged his shoulders.

"Pa, when were ya here last time?"

"Why's it matter?"

"It just does."

Pa rubbed his forehead before answering. "The day before you ate supper at Ben and Katherine's."

The day before he'd proposed.

"Thank you, Pa." The man nodded.

"Son, we can stand here and talk or get to work. Looks like the screen came loose since I was here. You can start with that."

Henry and Pa made their way toward the back of the house while Wallace carried in the boxes for Ma. When he set down the last one, he finally allowed himself to take in the scene of the front room. The outline of picture frames on the wallpaper testified to its yellowing, but small cobwebs in the corner bragged of a short lifespan. He peeked into each room before returning to the front. Wallace sucked in a breath. Overall, the house and it's few contents appeared clean and kempt. He turned and bent to look his mother in the eye.

"Ma, you came here with Pa the other day, didn't you?"

"Might had." The woman was tying her blue floral duster over her dress. "You scoot on out. This is woman's work in here." Wallace hugged her then walked onto the front porch and grabbed a screwdriver from the tool bin Henry had unloaded there.

A couple of hours into the work, Wallace joined Henry at the sawhorse beside the shed. "Need help?" The man looked up then pointed to the hammer lying on the ground. "You hammer while I keep sawing. You might be good with an engine or a hunting gun, but I don't trust you with a saw." Henry laughed.

"That's a good sound."

"I had a tickle fight with my kids this morning. We were laughing and Lena was crying." Henry looked him in the eye. "She's a good woman, and I hate putting her through pain when I get this way."

"No more than she hates seeing you in pain, I reckon."

Henry paused, as though absorbing Wallace's words, then smiled. "I reckon."

They worked in friendly companionship. Wallace answering Henry's questions here and there about the garage. Lena had filled him in on the news. Wallace suspected Henry was being polite to not ask about Clara, but Wallace had a need to talk.

"I reckon it's good Clara said no. I got nothing to offer her."

"You got exactly what she needs. And I figure she's realizin' that even while she's traipsing around Austin." Wallace wanted to press Henry. What did he have that she needed? Love? Now that she'd gotten a taste of adventure, he feared his love wouldn't satisfy the longings placed in her by the Creator.

"I hope not. I don't want to disappoint her by not offering marriage again."

"Then offer it. You both need to come to your senses." Wallace grimaced at the hint of irritation in Henry's tone.

"You sound like Ben."

"When hard times come, you're gonna want the woman you love beside you. And Wallace, hard times are a sure thing."

Wallace couldn't deny the truth in his words.

An auto horn blasting drew their attention, and Wallace was relieved by the distraction. The men walked through weeds and sighted Ben's pickup bed overloaded with Williamses and Joneses of various size and ages. Clara's oldest brother had a lawnmower braced against him. Bodies bounded from every direction and scattered across the yard. Ma and Pa stepped off the porch. Had he been less acquainted with these families, he might suspect their intentions toward helping him were to prompt another proposal. Clara's family were here today because they were good folks. He rubbed the back of his neck. And perhaps they knew a bit more about what love is willing to sacrifice than he did.

"Howdy." Wallace trotted over to the truck bed and helped Jacob with the mower. Lena and her children had run to Henry. Wallace saw him kiss his wife, then pull his children into a hug. No doubt they needed assurance that Henry was doing fine. Hello, how-are-you, and let-me-help-you-with-that filled the air. Ben announced that Lena had prepared a feast while he and all the kids had helped Katherine with inventory at the store. "Now, everyone's here to pitch in." Ben smiled. Wallace breathed slowly. These were Clara's people. She was everywhere and nowhere at the same moment.

"I have a surprise." Katherine called a decibel above the chatter. "We got a postcard from Clara. It's from San Antonio."

Everywhere and nowhere. He ached with longing for her. How could he manage to live in this house, this town, and not have her for his wife?

God, please get me out of here.

His heart and head pronounced what others needn't hear while his face and words portrayed the opposite.

"So glad you're here."

Chapter 18
September 1937 | Layton, Texas

He could make it to their house after breakfast, he supposed. "Alright, I'll see you in the morning around nine." Standing in the church aisle, Amy Carlson shook her head no. "I won't hear of you coming to the parsonage that late eating who-knows-what for breakfast. Join us at eight for a home cooked meal. Wendell will enjoy your company." Wallace grinned and tilted his hat. "Eight it is."

The irony of the conversation amused Wallace. As far back as his childhood, Amy Carlson had driven an auto with enthusiasm and no fear. When a triple beep followed by a single beep sounded, those within earshot knew that Amy Carlson was behind the wheel driving past or pulling in. Indeed, the woman could most likely repair the "ting ting" she'd described to him. Either way, he realized the thought of spending her time bent over an auto or at the garage while he made repairs did not appeal to her. "With Maggie being sick, we're behind on getting the room ready for the interim preacher. I just finished putting up wallpaper last night." After the Saturday he'd had fixing up his own place, Wallace appreciated the woman's dilemma. "And Wendell is just too weak to drive and sit at the garage."

Wallace glanced around the small church. He treasured the worn pews saturated with the scent of Murphy's Oil Soap. He inhaled as a memory paraded past his heart.

"Maggie! Are you hurt?" Ten-year-old Clara's hand flew over her mouth, but a giggle still escaped despite the concern in her voice. Wallace refrained his own laughter as he moved toward the scene. Petite Maggie Carlson lay in a heap on the floor between two pews. Clara stood at one end of the pew while Mary Forder sat at the other. After church, he'd noticed the girls sliding across the slick pew, and Maggie paid for it with a bit of her dignity. "Here you go, Maggie." Wallace offered his hand and pulled her up. With pink cheeks, Maggie looked up at him and whispered a thank you. Clara grabbed her and hugged her. "Oh, Maggie, can you walk?" At that moment, Katherine Williams turned toward the commotion. "Clara Williams..." Wallace backed away and headed out the church door. He'd

heard enough to know that Clara had instigated the "grand" idea. He sure did like her spunk.

Maggie was nowhere in sight. "I don't see Maggie. Is she still sick?"

"No, she's recovered, but we wanted her to take another day and rest. But don't tell the pastor that." Amy laughed at her own joke.

Wallace didn't mind the thought of grabbing his tools and heading to the parsonage to work on their auto. After all, Pastor Wendell Carlson was a hunting partner and good friend, not to mention a good pastor. What he did mind is that Maggie would likely be home. He hadn't seen her since the evening he toted her to Ben and Katherine's house. Lena and Henry had agreed Henry should return to work, which meant the recovered stand-in didn't need to stand-in at all. He wouldn't change the situation though, so glad was he that Henry was trying to carry on with normal life.

After Amy walked off, Wallace moved away from the pew and caught up with Ma and Pa who were talking to Ben at the door. Once again, Ben Williams had delivered a fairly good sermon in Wendell's place. The man was liked and respected in town, with no wonder. He was good-hearted and hard-working. Ben was a faithful believer who never grew bored with God's story in his life. However, the man never claimed to be a preacher.

Wallace was in earshot of Ben's words with Pa. "I tell you, Pony, nobody's gonna be happier for the interim to get here than me. Lands sakes, I'm looking forward to hollering an amen instead of a sermon." Wallace laughed. Never had Ben hollered a sermon.

He made his way to Ma and Pa. With his obligation to Amy the next morning, his Sunday trip to Evan for a home cooked lunch would have to be a turn-around-one. Of his eight siblings, only two still lived at home. Both of them, Willy and Mamie, stood beside his car for the ride to Evan. Wallace tossed his key to William. "You're behind the wheel, baby brother." Six years younger than he, Clara's age, Willy was a couple of inches shorter than him, but just as broad. Other than Wallace's statement beard, they resembled one another.

Monday morning rolled around, and Wallace took the last slurp of his coffee, hoping it would appease his growling stomach that was used to eating before eight o'clock. His eye moved to the San Antonio postcard lying near his Bible. He blew out a breath, picking up the scent of coffee it emitted. Katherine had meant well when she handed him Clara's postcard. "Keep this for us, Wallace." He'd balked. "It's yours. I have a letter from her." Katherine had pointed to the address. "Says Family and Friends. I think that qualifies you."

He slid the postcard beneath his Bible where her letter rested. A sharp pain filled his chest. He missed Clara. "Get used to it." Does one ever get used to pain? He reckoned not. Perhaps one shifts it around to balance the weight.

Some moments he felt smothered by regret over not asking her again to marry him on the morning they parted. Yet, if she had left with a promise between them, how would he handle his current financial situation once she returned? She'd be expecting to plan a wedding while he would be planning to break her heart because he couldn't provide for her. On the other hand, he was right to refute proposing again at that moment. She needed to know whether she loved him or the idea of him. He needed to know that too.

And how did she feel about Andrew Slayton? He needed to know that too.

He stepped into the garage and took his tool box from the shelf. He'd grown into manhood here. The circumstances and conversations that had matured him lingered here. He'd be packing them up for future use when he left this place. He'd need their wisdom.

A bright, cool day greeted him as he drove with one hand on the wheel the other thumbing a rhythm on the seat. Hundreds of miles from him Clara must be starting her day. What did it hold for her, and who would be a part of the happenings? Andrew Slayton?

He jolted at a realization. He'd never had to feel jealous over Clara. This wasn't pride, but simple observation. As Clara matured, those young men who knew them both must have also known her heart would be his. Lands sake, outside the confines of their town, the assumption that had been unspoken seemed somehow silenced. Out from under the assumption, Clara may find another far more appealing than him.

He knocked on the parsonage door and Wendell greeted him. Wallace didn't give much thought to men's appearances, but there was no doubting that Wendell Carlson had been a handsome man, yet he stood before him now gaunt and weak. Traces of his familiar features could be seen under the veil of pale skin. Wallace would be relieved for him when the interim arrived.

"Morning Wallace. Come on in." The men shook hands. "Morning, Pastor." Wallace moved inside the familiar setting. He'd first come here with Pa and Ben Williams to pick up Pastor for rabbit hunting. He'd been struck by the sight of a curved black piano in the corner of the front room. It filled most of the space, save a sofa and table. Young Maggie had slipped onto the seat and plunked out the tune of a hymn.

At the moment Maggie's fingers were flitting over the keys producing a tune Wallace didn't recognize, but enjoyed hearing. The sight of her, enveloped in the music she played, struck him. He released the image of her sick and replaced it with this one. She'd make a lovely wife for some man, but not him.

Wallace didn't realize until she stopped playing that the music had been a buffer for his awkwardness around her. Her previous words swam in his head, exaggerating their own intentions. "If I weren't sick, I'd kiss you. Consider yourself kissed." He refrained from shaking his head in an attempt to ward off the memory. As ill as she'd been, he wondered if she recalled saying that to him.

Amy Carlson announced from the dining room that breakfast was ready. Maggie rose from the piano bench and their eyes made contact. A pink hue flashed on her cheeks, but gave no distinction between embarrassment or attraction. They moved together toward the table.

"Good morning, Wallace."

"Hello, Maggie."

"I'm glad to see you. I haven't been able to thank you for helping me."

"No thanks needed. It's nice to see you feeling good."

He pulled out her chair then went to sit across from her in the chair her brother indicated. She sat in front of a large window with a silhouette of the church behind it. He'd be facing her throughout the meal. The parsonage was a small house by original design, aged by the men of God and their families who'd sought solace here. Amy's brother was a wealthy businessman whose contributions to their work over the years included enlarging and enhancing the home, transforming it into a place the Carlsons could welcome congregates with a meal or refuge.

The family clasped hands and prayed. Now he felt relief that Maggie was seated across from him rather than beside him.

The heap of food on Wallace's plate wasn't there long. He was glad he'd come hungry. He pushed away from the table and stood with Wendell, grabbing his tool box as they headed outside. During the meal Maggie behaved as Clara's friend the way he'd always known her, speculating about the adventures she and Mary might be up to; yet, Wallace was relieved to be outside, away from her. Wendell leaned against the car as Wallace inspected it.

"Pastor, reckon Henry's really feeling good enough to run the store?"

"I suppose no one knows better than him."

"I reckon. Pains me to see him feel low. He's so good-hearted and happy usually."

"It's that good heart and his faith that gives me hope when his mind struggles. "

Wallace dropped a wrench, and Wendell bent to pick it up. The man's hand was clammy when Wallace retrieved it from him. "Head back in the house Wendell." Pastor didn't argue. Wallace settled back into his work, heedless of the minutes passing yet aware that each one was being spent apart from Clara. He ached for her.

The click of the front door caused Wallace to look up from the engine and wipe his hands on the rag hanging out his pocket. He stretched then spoke before turning is eyes toward the one approaching.

"Wendell?"

"I brought you some sweet tea."

Maggie.

"Thank you." He took the glass, careful to not touch her fingers in the process.

She leaned against the auto just as her father had done. Her perfume was light and floral.

"Can you fix it?"

"Yessum. I'm about done." He gulped the tea, emptying the glass then handed it to her. "Thank you." He looked back inside the engine.

She took the glass, but not the hint.

"I hear you worked on your new place."

"Yep."

It was seconds before she spoke.

"With Clara gone, I'd be happy to help you put things in order."

"Thanks, but no need. Ma, Lena, and Katherine already got me set up."

She moved to stand beside him. He felt her hand on his arm. Her touch was unwelcome.

"Wallace, look at me."

He did.

"I'm sure you remember what I said to you the other night."

She paused, but he didn't step into it. Instead, he pulled his arm away from her hand.

"Wallace, I'm sorry I said it."

"You were real sick with fever and not thinking straight. I know you didn't mean it."

Her eyes welled up.

"No, I was thinking straight. I meant what I said. I care about you. That's why I'm sorry I said it."

Some confusing sense of compassion came over him.

"Maggie."

"Wallace, I know who owns your heart. But do you own hers?"

He wished he did so he could marry her. He wished he didn't because he couldn't marry her.

"Maggie, you're a fine young woman, and,"

"And a good young woman, so I'll keep my feelings in their place for safe keeping until the time is right."

"Until the man is right. I'm not him."

"I can hope."

"Don't."

Tears slipped down her cheeks. He hadn't wanted to hurt her, but she needed the freedom truth would bring.

"You deserve a man who isn't in love with someone else."

"You might grow to love me."

"I wouldn't. Maggie, your thirst to be loved would never be satisfied by me. Your spirit would dry up. I won't do that to you."

She wiped tears from her cheeks. He stared as she muffled a sob, dried her eyes, and took a deep breath before opening the front door and walking through.

He finished the repair then said his thank-yous and good-byes to Wendell and Amy. His stubborn eyes roamed the house looking for her. Maggie was nowhere in sight. Wendell wrinkled his forehead, but Wallace couldn't determine his inquiry. He hoped Wendell was baffled over his hasty departure and not the hasty retreat his daughter must have made when she'd entered the house.

"I've got somewhere else I need to be."

Somewhere was anywhere but here.

Wallace pulled open his auto door and slipped into the seat. He needed to shake the conversation with Maggie, but concern prevented it. He blew out a breath. His determination to not marry Clara would alter his standing with Ben. How aware were Wendell and Amy of Maggie's attraction to him? In rejecting her, had he threatened his friendship with them?

Women!

The shadows settling into the room caught his eye. He glanced at the clock advertising Sinclair motor oil and smirked. He needed to replace the old thing hanging over the desk. A shattered cover forced him to squint at the time. Mid-afternoon. Lunchtime had slipped by unnoticed. He'd tinkered around the garage and stalled long enough. He best gather the last of his things and head to his house for supper. His mouth watered at the thought of Ma's fried chicken sitting in his icebox. He'd left her house yesterday loaded with canned goods, baked goods, and the chicken. There was no reason he shouldn't move on and sit at his small table in his small kitchen in his small house that was too big for one person but just the right size to start a family.

In three strides he stood before the wire that served as his clothes closet. A grasp with both hands and he'd collected all his clothes. He looked around the room verifying he'd packed all his other belongings. Holding the clothes hangers in his hands, Wallace pulled the door nearly shut with his foot. He sniffed. The scent of home had been comprised of all things auto for years. Wallace wondered what odors would linger in his new place.

Did loneliness have a scent?

He looked at the nail hanging beside the shelf to make sure he'd hung his room key there then moved past the desk. The arm of his coat on the hanger caught the telephone, knocking it to the floor. Ugh! Wallace dropped his clothes and bent to pick up the telephone. He sucked in air when a compulsion to call Clara slammed into him. As though the phone were on fire, he shot up, threw the black contraption on the desk, and like a crazed man, he yanked open the desk draw and began to shove items aside.

It had been a couple of years since he'd looked at the thin pocket-sized notepad, but Wallace recalled scribbling "Garrett Forder, Austin" and a corresponding telephone number on it. The man had reported for his first year in the legislature and had left his auto behind for a simple repair. Wallace and he had communicated via telephone during the transaction.

Ouch! Something sharp nicked him. He yanked his finger to his mouth and tasted blood. His eyes spotted an old, open pocket knife that likely had been found in the garage but not claimed. He picked it up to look for rust and saw none. Relieved, he tossed the knife into the metal bucket serving as a trashcan. Another shuffling around in the drawer revealed the notepad. He thumbed through the pages and found his notation. Sweat beaded on his brow and his breathing quickened. He set the phone upright and dialed.

"Forder residence." He recognized Abigail's voice.

"Hello, Mrs. Forder, this is Wallace James."

A slight gasp reached his ears.

"Wallace, hello. Is everyone well in Layton?"

"Yes." Except Henry. But that was another conversation.

"How is Pastor?"

"Weak, but he's improving. The interim is coming tomorrow."

"That's good."

"Can I speak with Clara?"

"Wallace, I'm sorry but she is not here." Disappointment squeezed his chest. "The tutor, Mr. Slayton, has taken Madie to the library." He fisted his hand when Andrew was mentioned. "Cass, Mary, and Clara went along, of course. Then…"

Mrs. Forder cut off her words, leaving an awkward pause. Jealousy filled the void. He was becoming familiar with the feeling. Wallace suspected Abigail did him a favor by cutting off her explanation.

"I see. Will you tell her I telephoned just to say hello?"

"She'll be sorry she missed you."

He wondered if that was true.

Wallace was certain he spoke cordialities and inquiries before hanging up the telephone, but he didn't hear the answers above the shouting of his thoughts. Calling for her stirred up a heap of emotions in his own soul. They trampled him like children running wild in a sunlit field. He'd have a difficult time gathering them back inside the cold, dark corner of his heart.

"You're a fool, Wallace James. Let the woman be."

He gathered his clothes and tossed them into his Plymouth before locking up the garage.

His head rested on the steering wheel. Wallace wept. Unashamedly.

Chapter 19

He stood so close she could feel his breath. The others waited in the auto, surely watching their interaction on the porch. Clara felt as though she were on display in one of Joske's Department Store windows. Andrew had drawn her aside when she set out to get in the auto. "My words and actions at the restaurant were wrong. I apologize for them." He rubbed her angel kiss with his finger. Clara noted he was looking directly into her eyes. *Perhaps Andrew Slayton can redeem himself after all.* Just as that thought settled in, another tapped her on the shoulder and cautioned her against the attraction.

Andrew's glasses enhanced eyes the color of bluebonnets below the swoop of black hair. He appeared vulnerable, yet she mustn't be gullible. She would forgive him, then keep him at a distance. After his abrupt departure Friday, her weekend had been free of his presence, and he seemed a figment of her girlish imagination. She'd found her thoughts turning to Wallace more than any other time since she'd arrived in Austin.

"I accept your apology." Clara turned and placed a foot on the front step, and felt Andrew's tug on her elbow. He attempted to place her hand through the crook in his arm. Clara pulled away. "As you wish." Andrew's tone contradicted the smile on his lips.

Clara squeezed into the back seat next to Madie who sat next to Mary. Cass occupied the front seat. She settled her purse on her lap and felt the bulk of her butterfly book and a small tablet stuffed inside. The trip to the library was to be followed by a trip to Barton Springs near the river. Clara hoped such a setting would inspire a story. Since she'd determined her creativity was tethered to the butterfly book, she brought along the treasure.

She'd chosen to wear her blue trousers and cream blouse for this outing, similar to how Mary and Cass were dressed. The style was new to Clara and felt as strange as her short haircut. She tugged on the navy cloth and adjusted her seating. Madie giggled.

"These are nothing like the overalls I wore as a girl." Clara winked at Madie.

"I think all you ladies look as cute as a bug's ear."

Mary laughed at the metaphor. Clara grinned at a memory.

"Mr. Slayton, do bugs really have ears?" Madie leaned forward to ask the question.

"You should try to find a book about that at the library."

"Mr. Slayton, do I have to? Sir." The young girl slammed her body back into the seat to enhance her disdain.

"No. But bugs ears are interesting. I wonder if Miss Clara has studied them."

His glance came her way. The smile on her lips had nothing to do with Andrew. Indeed, she had read about bug ears, as Madie called them, and it had been Wallace who'd shown her the information. She'd wanted to kiss him that day, not from gratitude, but from deep attraction. Instead, she'd tamped her emotions with a hug much like a sister.

"Clara, you write bug stories. Do bugs have ears?"

"No, but they hear other ways."

"Remember her story about Grady the Grasshopper?" Cass turned to face her daughter.

Madie squealed out a yes, then proceeded to tell the story as though none of them had heard it. Only one had not, and he kept glancing back to the author. Clara turned her head and faced Madie more directly, wondering if Andrew was hearing a word the girl was saying and wishing that Wallace were in the driver's seat sending glances her way.

Clara tried all morning to imagine such a large building filled with books. The sight was more than she had conjured up. She bounced on the balls of her feet and tried to contain her curiosity as she stood inside the library. She took in the scene and hoped she would be able to describe this place to Aunt Lena.

"I wish I were allowed to take photographs in here." Andrew grinned at all four of the females staring at their surroundings. "I'd capture the look of amazement on your faces."

He led Cass and Madie to the children's room while Mary and Clara sought out their own selections. Now seated at a table across from them, Mary thumbed through a book on the history of fashion while Clara read the history of the Alamo.

She'd grown used to his presence in the home and the interaction between Andrew and Madie during their daily tutoring sessions. Until the incident at lunch on Friday, a playful ease and attraction lingered between them. It had left Clara trying to temper her curiosity about Andrew and the life he represented against Wallace and the life she knew. And loved. She had to admit, seeing Andrew in this setting, keeping Madie engaged in learning, was a pleasure to watch. Andrew was at his best when he tutored, she supposed. Yet, unlike watching Wallace in his garage, observing Andrew here did not bring the sense of belonging that Clara felt there.

Mary's whisper broke Clara's thoughts. "Andrew only has eyes for you." Clara stifled a laugh, then whispered an altered version of the Texas University theme song in Mary's ear. "The eyes of Andrew are upon you." Mary didn't attempt to cover her laugh, breaking the silence in the room. The man himself looked their way, and Clara caught his puzzled look. She waved her hands to dismiss him. He smiled and winked before putting a finger in front of his mouth to indicate silence.

Clara considered dear Mary. Even now when she imagined confiding about Andrew's actions at lunch, Clara felt awkward. To her knowledge, Mary, Maggie, and her had not kept secrets from one another. Well, except for one. Clara noticed the way Maggie had begun looking at Wallace in the last year. Clara and Maggie had an unspoken understating that neither would speak of her attraction to Wallace.

They left the library mid-afternoon and stopped for ice cream before heading to Barton Springs. The weather was too chilly for swimming, but Mary had assured her the view at the springs would be worth her time. The sky threatened rain and sent a light breeze to tickle Clara's skin.

As she sat on a blanket by the water, her writing tablet nearby, Clara looked through the pages of her butterfly book to find the one blank page she'd discovered two days ago. Yet, her hands kept turning until she reached the last page where the Wallace and Clara butterflies were drawn.

Andrew appeared from behind and came to stand in front of her. His actions toward her this afternoon had been no different than those toward Mary, and Clara was grateful. He called out her name, getting her attention, then took a photograph before sitting down next to her. She closed the book when she'd sensed his approach.

His arm brushed against hers when he pointed to the butterfly book.

"Who's Wallace?"

"What?"

"Wallace and Clara. I saw the drawing."

He was bold. She would be too.

"He's the man who proposed to me."

She felt his slight jerk.

"Yet, you're not wearing a ring. So you are not engaged?"

"No."

"So, I might have miss-stepped with you, but I didn't step over another man's line."

"No." You stepped over my line.

"You're a character in a real broken-hearted romance story."

Story. If he only knew that the reason she was here beside him and not with Wallace had everything to do with a story.

"My question is, which of us is the antagonist? Wallace or me?"

She covered her ears. "Stop exaggerating, Andrew."

"Clara Williams, you're intriguing."

Before she could reply, he popped up and moved toward the water.

✦ ✦ ✦

An hour later they pulled into the driveway. Garrett's auto and another were parked outside the house. Clara thought the other belonged to Porter Franklin. Mary's squeal confirmed her suspicion.

Andrew beeped the horn, and before they could crawl from the auto, both Garrett and Porter appeared on the front porch. A mist filled the air and the riders scurried to the front porch. Porter welcomed Mary home and

Garrett hugged both his wife and daughter. Mrs. Forder appeared behind the screen door. Her lovely face brightened by a smile.

"Ladies, we've got a surprise for you." Garrett's eyes roved over the group. "Freshen up from your adventures then hurry and eat the sandwich waiting for you in the kitchen. We're all taking Mother to the cinema."

"Me too?" Garrett knelt to address Madie. "No, but Cibby is coming over and expects you to help make cookies and eat some." Garrett tweaked his daughter's nose.

"Cookies for supper." Madie rubbed her stomach. "No, a sandwich for supper." Garrett replied with mock irritation. Madie giggled. "I know."

"Mrs. Abigail, did you know about this?" Cass inquired as she walked through the door. "Only long enough to help Porter with the sandwich fixins' he brought. The menfolk planned all this."

One look at Andrew's expression, and Clara knew he was part of the menfolk. He raised his eyebrows and smiled at her.

Mary ran a brush through her hair. "Do you think Porter will sit next to me? Oh my, he may hold my hand." Clara wasn't sure about the hand holding, but she suspected Porter would have no other seat but the one beside Mary. "I think you'll sit between your mother and your brother." Clara patted her friend's shoulder and noted her disappointed expression. "Lands sake, Mary. Relax. Of course Porter will want to sit next to you. Why else would he be making sandwiches and taking your mother to a movie? You silly thing."

Clara suspected one assumption resembled another, and Andrew would be seated next to her.

"You're frowning. Don't you want to go to the movie, Clara?"

"Yes, of course." I just don't want to be so close to Andrew especially in the dark. The words were for her mind only. Now was not the time for Mary to know how she felt.

Following a flurry of activity, Clara found herself seated again in the backseat of Andrew's auto. Mrs. Forder graced the front passenger seat while the tutor followed behind Garrett's car where the rest of the group rode. Clara suspected Mary was fuming that Cass was seated beside her because both men rode up front. Clara wondered if Mary realized the role of protective father now fell on her brother.

The drivers parked and passengers unloaded.

"Line up for a photograph under the flashing sign." Andrew adjusted his camera and aimed at the group who chuckled as they settled into position. "Porter, look at the camera. Not the person next to you." The young senator stood on the end beside Mary. While others laughed, Clara wished Wallace were posed next to her. She supposed Mrs. Forder wished the same about her husband.

The aroma of popped corn captivated Clara the moment she stepped into the carpeted theater with chandeliers hanging overhead. Andrew placed a warm bag into her hand while juggling another plus two sodas. Clara received it and smiled, despite the nagging weight constant generosity sent her way. She knew that no obligations came with what the Forders gave, and she wished to give in return somehow; however, she suspected Andrew may want something in return for his generosity that she was unwilling to give.

Clara slipped a crunchy kernel onto her tongue as the group moved in single file down the aisle. What a relief that Andrew's hands were full and he couldn't guide her with his fingers against her back. Garrett turned into a row and counted down seven seats before settling in. One by one the party settled in the next seat. A knot formed in Clara's stomach. She would be seated between Mary and Andrew who would get the end seat. Mary would be focused on Porter. No doubt Andrew would be focused on Clara. Coincidence or collaboration?

The lights dimmed and the curtains raised, revealing the screen. Joan Crawford in the Bride Wore Red.

As the plot unfolded, Clara slumped in her seat. She determined she didn't like the movie. A girl of modest means masquerading as moneyed. Small town girl turns socialite. Did anyone else in her party see the irony? While the question teased her, Andrew's arm brushed against her as he placed it over the top of her seat and leaned in. With his height and that position, Clara felt dominated by his presence.

"You smell good." His lips brushed her ear. His fingers rubbed her shoulder.

Apparently the irony hadn't occurred to Andrew. Maybe when the lights came on, she'd have popcorn stuck in her teeth, and he would flee, disgusted.

She controlled her giggle at the thought. Clara shifted her shoulder away from Andrew and glanced at Porter who had both hands in his lap, apparently behaving as a gentleman. Perhaps Andrew understood her hint, for his slender fingers slipped from her shoulder. Wallace never took such liberties even when she'd suggested it. *I'd like nothing better than to kiss you. And if you were rightly mine, I would.*

The time was after ten o'clock when Clara stomped her muddy feet on the front porch. Why had she worn her trousers? The hem was soaked from rain. She handed Andrew his umbrella before darting into the Forder's front room. Garrett released the screen he was holding open and slipped in behind her. She heard him lock it. Lightening brightened the sky. Mary pulled away from the front window where she'd been waving good-bye to Porter. Garrett said his good nights and headed to the bedrooms where the others already gone.

"I'm crazy over Porter." Mary's arm slipped through Clara's. They turned toward the bedroom hallway. "I'm guessing he's crazy about you too." Mary's sigh was far from subtle. They both jerked at a light knock on the front door. Mary moved to peek out the window. "It's Andrew."

With that, Mary winked at Clara and headed back toward their room. Frustrated, Clara felt she had no choice but to open the door. She did and slipped onto the porch, shutting the door behind her and easing the screen.

"Andrew." He stood there wet, the umbrella closed in his hand. "You left your purse in my car." She glanced at his other hand and knew it would not be holding her bag because she hadn't brought it to the movie.

"No, I didn't."

"No, you didn't." His voice was deep with a compelling tone that sent a shudder over her skin.

Clara reached for the screen door, but Andrew took her hand, and in a swift motion pulled her body against his and locked her in his arms, keeping her own trapped between them.

His head lowered toward hers. "I'm going to kiss you." His mouth was hot against her own. As she squirmed, his lips pressed deeper. Possession was in his kiss. Clara groaned against the force, frightened by the feel of him against her. A scream moved through her throat, and he must have felt it, for in one motion he pulled away and covered her mouth with his hand.

129

"You asked me where I went that night in San Antonio. There are places a man can get what he needs from a woman, and that's where I went. But I'm charmed by your goodness and would much rather get what I want from you." He pulled his hand away just enough to pat her lips. "We could slip away. I'd share my needs with you."

Her skin grew clammy as a memory resurrected itself.

"Come sit in my lap, Clara, and let me hug you. A hand belonging to a man pulled on her four-year-old fingers. She shook her head back and forth while she fought the urge to wet her overalls. "I don't want to, Uncle Joe."

"But I take care of you and love you, even with your ugly mark."

"Please don't make me, Uncle Joe. I think you're a bad man, not a good one."

His face contorted, and he grabbed her teddy bear before shoving her in the corner of his workshop.

"Sit! Even your Papa doesn't love his ugly daughter." Indeed, Papa was never around to protect her.

Clara swallowed her gorge. *Uncle Joe.* The once shadowy image now glared at her in full color. He had not been good man, and neither was the attractive one holding her captive.

Clara pushed against Andrew with her shoulder, managing to free one arm.

"You are not a good person."

"No one is perfect, Clara."

"No, but some are good. I know good. I've looked it in the eye. I've seen its smile. Heard its laughter."

"You are in quite a predicament being held by me, but talking poetically about another."

"Let go of me!" She managed to pull her hand back far enough to slap him. "I'm telling the Forders about your behavior."

Andrew jerked and released her except for his hand gripping her wrist. "If you go tattling, you'll only make yourself look foolish and loose. After all, I'm the good-natured tutor and the son in a respected Austin family." He grabbed her hair and jerked her head backward. "You're just a naive girl, Clara. A little pet to the Forders. I found your naivety appealing at first. At the moment it sickens me."

He released her. As rain pelted the porch, Andrew stormed to his auto. Clara stifled her sobs. Perhaps Andrew was right and her reputation would be marred with the Forders. She must have brought his behavior on herself. She couldn't risk the friendship her family had with the Forders by telling them about him. Her shoulders sagged. What shame had she brought upon her friends and family?

The bedroom door creaked when she opened it, and Mary's voice floated through the dark.

"What did Andrew want?"

Clara eased toward the dresser. She could hear Madie's breathing as she slept next to Mary.

"He thought I left my purse at the theater. He didn't see me carry it in the house before he left. He offered to go back for it."

She despised lying.

The taste of cola and popcorn rose to her throat. She swallowed it.

"Oh. Did you leave it there?"

"No. I left it here. Sweet dreams, Mary."

"You too. We'll gossip tomorrow."

Clara fumbled around her drawer to find her bed clothes, then tiptoed to the bathroom and changed. She could no longer hold in the emotions causing her body to tremble and ran water to muffle the sobs. Her privacy was cut short by a gentle knock on the bathroom door. Dread surged through her. Who had heard her crying and what would she say to them? She splashed water on her face, then dabbed it with a towel. The mirror reflected a distraught young woman.

"Clara?" She recognized Mrs. Forder's voice.

"I'll be right out."

Clara tightened her robe around her, grabbed her clothes, and opened the door, wondering how much she should tell Mrs. Forder about Andrew's behavior if she inquired.

"I know it's late, but I haven't had a chance to tell you this." Clara adjusted mentally. Perhaps Mrs. Forder had not heard her crying. "Wallace James telephoned for you this afternoon."

Clara gasped at the blinding truth. She was hopelessly in love with Wallace and had been since—she knew not when. Some unmarked moment no doubt.

"I thought you'd like to know. He said everyone is well. He simply wanted to tell you hello." Tears paraded down Clara's cheeks. "Oh, sweet dear. I know what it's like to miss someone terribly." Of course she did. Mason had been gone less than a year. Clara felt selfish.

Abigail pulled Clara close and hugged her. Like Momma. Sobs begged to be released, but were held back by pursed lips. "The telephone is right there. It will be good for you to hear from home. Call the garage."

"It won't be improper?"

"I doubt he would think that." Abigail patted her hair. "Do you know the number to ring?"

"Yes." By heart.

"Just talk quietly. I'll see you in the morning."

She nodded her thanks.

Clara set her clothes in a chair, then picked up the receiver with trembling fingers. Miles from her, yet Wallace had reached out when she needed him.

Seven rings and no answer. It was almost eleven at night. Wallace made a habit of being in bed by ten. But, no doubt, if he were there in the small side room, he could hear the office telephone ringing.

Clara's lips trembled. Where was Wallace James this late Monday night? She listened as the telephone continued to ring, the sound as close to home and to him as she could be.

At last, the operator broke in.

Clara hung up the receiver. "I love you."

Chapter 20

EARLY OCTOBER 1937 | LAYTON, TEXAS

"**Clara.**" He lifted his arm from his chest and let it flop to the other side of the bed. The sheet felt cold and unrumpled. She wasn't there. She had never been there. A sadness moved through him. She never would be there.

The arm sprung back and plopped across his face. His fingers rubbed against the stiff whiskers. He'd grown the beard as a statement against being separated from Clara. Now that his life would not be spent with her, he reckoned he'd keep the beard as a statement of the solitary man he now was, but never wished to be.

Wallace grunted and sat up. What bleak thoughts for beginning a Tuesday morning. God gave him breath, but for the life of him, Wallace didn't know what the Good Lord planned to do with it.

Well, except for today. Today he was to get up and run the garage, go home, and then do it all again tomorrow until the garage closed the door on the todays. A smile snuck its way to his face. Wallace had to admit his work fulfilled him. He'd best be grateful for the time he had left at Myers.

He made his way to the bathroom, glad Ma's cousin had installed indoor plumbing. Grooming behind him, he stomped his way to the kitchen, because he could, and started percolating the coffee. Rummaging through the ice box, he discovered the apple pound cake Ma had brought on Saturday. That would do. No need to fry up bacon and eggs. His first breakfast in his house would satisfy his sweet tooth. Ah. Home sweet home.

The coffee stopped bubbling having filled his house with a delicious aroma. He poured black liquid into his cup and held a big piece of cake in his hand. No need to dirty a plate and fork when his fingers would do.

The driver's seat of his Plymouth welcomed him. With one hand on the wheel and the other dangling outside the window, Wallace drove to Myers Garage and pulled in. His mechanic's 1925 Ford was parked outside the building. Wallace glanced at his watch, certain he wasn't late. Indeed, for the first time since he'd been hired, his mechanic arrived on time. Wallace wondered if he was also trying to make the most of the days left in the

133

business. A running motor behind him drew Wallace's attention. He stepped from his auto and waved. He could always count on the retired school teacher to arrive first thing when she needed repairs. He blew out a breath and closed his car door. The air felt cool, but heavy. He reckoned the gray clouds would exhale rain any moment.

The door to one of the repair bays opened as his mechanic rolled the chain then motioned her to pull forward. Wallace unlocked the office door and stepped inside and noticed the telephone. For the second time in a short morning he felt a wave of sadness move over him. Yesterday he'd longed to hear her voice through the receiver when he called. Perhaps he should try again now before she got too busy in her day. Tomorrow she was to see the publisher. He could say he was calling to wish her well. He reached toward the device then jerked his hand back. No. He needed to let Clara be. No well wishes. No marriage. After all most likely, he'd soon have no money.

He opened the door to the garage itself.

"Morning, Miss Henderson. Coffee?"

"Why, good morning, Wallace. No thank you. My brother will be here soon to get me.

"Yessum."

"Anyone heard from little Clara Williams?"

Wallace rolled his eyes. Time must have stopped for Miss Henderson in 1930 when she retired, leaving her students in perpetual grade school.

"Her parents got a post card."

"Bless her sweet heart." Indeed.

He nodded and closed the door.

Wallace set out to count inventory. He reckoned, if Mr. Myers didn't mind, he'd offer to let Henry buy some of the stocked goods to keep on hand at the store once the garage closed. He figured it was the least he could do for his customers. Henry had a knack for autos, so he'd be able to sell the merchandise well.

Most likely, Henry would offer Wallace a job selling the stuff himself, but the thought of seeing Clara at the store with any frequency would make accepting that offer impossible. He grunted. Why, he'd have the same issue with church. Lands sakes. Now he'd have to travel miles every Sunday to worship at another church. His head ached at the thought, but it would go against his nature to cause any discomfort to Clara with his presence. He sighed. Maybe he'd be causing her discomfort with his lack of presence. He really didn't know if she'd return from Austin hoping to marry him or hoping to dismiss him.

The morning was busy, as Tuesday was half-price day on oil. Wallace closed the hood on his third car for the morning, trying to ignore the growl in his stomach. His sugary breakfast had worn off a couple of hours ago. "You bring your lunch?" His mechanic grunted a yes. He washed his hands and face, then made his way to the diner. Water dripped from his beard. The aroma of meatloaf accosted Wallace as he pushed through the door.

"Henry!"

"Afternoon. Lena's back cooking in the kitchen."

"Don't I know it!"

Katherine stuck her head out the doorway to the store's back office, then waved at him. For the length of a breath, he thought his world had gathered itself back into place. In the next, he felt Clara's absence.

Within moments Lena sat a plate of warm meatloaf in front of him and another across from him. "You joining me?" Lena smiled. "No, I'm working my fingers to the bones. He's joining you." She titled her head backward. Wallace looked to see Henry coming his way. He kissed his wife on the cheek, then sat down. Good. Wallace would present his merchandise idea to him.

"May I?"

Wallace nodded. Henry asked the blessing.

"Let's talk business, Wallace."

"I'm losing mine."

"Exactly. Perfect timing."

"For what?"

"To open our used auto store."

"No." Wallace took his first bite.

"I'm going to the bank tomorrow to request a loan."

Henry had mentioned nothing about these plans Saturday when they'd done repairs at his new house. Was this a whim?

"Think about the economy. Henry have you lost your mind?"

"A bit." Henry laughed and choked on his food.

Wallace could feel his face heating up. He'd not intended to make a pun over Henry's condition.

"Relax, Wallace. I know the idea sounds crazy, but trust me, I'm not thinking crazy. I talked to Lena and to Ben about this a couple of months ago. With Myers going up for sale, we figured the time might be right to move forward."

Wallace sipped his sweet tea then cleared his throat. "Could you handle being rejected?"

"You sound like Lena." He tapped on the table. "Yes. And the point is, I'd borrow enough to start up business and then pay it back with profit. If things didn't work out, I got enough set aside from my Pa's inheritance to pay the loan back on my own if I had to. I'd need someone to repair the autos, someone to paint 'em. and someone to sale 'em. You'd have your pick of the jobs."

"Who's to say Walter will sell the garage to you at the cost of his loan. That arrangement was with me. He's probably got buyers who could pay more than you."

"I know. That's a conversation I'll have with Walter once I talk to the bank."

"It's none of my business, but why'd Lena agree to this."

"Because she thinks it will work. Myer's Garage is the perfect spot."

"Henry," Wallace put down his fork and leaned in toward his friend, "is this charity?" Perhaps his friend wasn't thinking straight. He'd need to check with Lena.

"I'm not that generous. It's business, and I want you to be a part of it, like we've always planned."

"We planned a partnership."

"That could come in time."

"And I need time to think about this."

"I'll give you until tomorrow." Henry grinned. "Fair enough. Take some days to think and pray."

"I was gonna suggest you buy some of the garage merchandise and sell it here." Wallace shrugged. "A lot less financial risk."

Something about Henry's offer nagged at Wallace. Despite the denial, the arrangement felt like charity, and risky charity at that. Wondering if Lena and Ben were appeasing Henry in his current state of mind also nagged at him. No, Wallace knew he wanted no part in the arrangement. And then there was the matter of Clara, who would certainly visit Henry at the auto shop.

He pushed his plate aside. The food had soured in his stomach.

"Lay out your inventory and prices for me. That idea will work even with the auto store open."

Wallace noticed Henry glance at the door. "Do you know that man who just walked in?"

Wallace turned that direction. A young stranger dressed in a suit stood at the counter, seeming to search for assistance. "No. He looks misplaced." Henry excused himself.

Wallace paid the bill then headed to where Henry stood next to the man.

"Reverend Campbell, meet Wallace James. Wallace, meet Graham Campbell, the interim preacher."

Wallace willed his jaw not to drop. The man before him looked no older than, well, than himself. It occurred to Wallace that preachers weren't born grown up, but he'd expected someone older. He had a good feeling the Carlsons did too.

"Nice to meet you. From Fredericksburg, right?"

"Yes. I just drove in. I'm to meet the Reverend Carlson here."

As though the scene had been rehearsed, the bell on the door jingled as the Carlson's walked in and paused.

"How about lunch, Reverend? On the house. Is your family in the auto?"

"Oh, no. It's just me. I'm not married."

Henry and the interim had their backs to the door, unaware of the Carlson's entrance. Wallace smiled. "Reverend Carlson." Henry turned.

"Wendell, just in time. Meet Reverend Graham Campbell. Graham, this is Reverend Carlson and his family."

Wendell and Amy were fine people. Wallace admired their composure as they met the young man, and even more so when they introduced him to Maggie. From the flush on both the young folk's faces, Wallace surmised that his concerns over Maggie had just ended and the Carlson's concerns had just begun.

He excused himself and two hours back into his work, the telephone rang in the office. "Myer's Garage."

The one-sided conversation with Walter made Wallace numb. He hung up the telephone and plopped into the desk chair, shaking his head back and forth. Tomorrow he'd be traveling to Sulphur Springs for a job interview. "Your reputation has spread all the way to Hopkins County. I arranged for you to meet the garage owner at noon tomorrow." Walter had been shrewd enough to build in a caveat. "Of course, he agreed you'd have until the end of the month to accept, knowing I offered you the garage."

And I promised Clara I'd be here when she returned. Was his integrity reason enough to keep that promise?

Sulphur Springs. Miles from the garage, the church, the store, his family, his friends, and Clara. Bearded Wallace could begin the new life he'd never wanted.

The thought intrigued him. He bent over the desk and laid his head on his arms. The thought also saddened him.

"Dear God, I want you to guide me, but I don't enjoy this uphill climb." Temptation taunted him. Call Clara. Wish her luck. Let her voice wash over you. Hear the emotions she speaks. Or doesn't speak.

The lightening crackled and thunder sounded. Within seconds, rain pelted against the building. Wallace exhaled. At times, he couldn't bear the sound of rain.

"There's no need for him to stay in my room at the garage. Let him use the spare room at my house." Wednesday morning rain hollered outside, so Wallace pulled the pastor into the office. Wendell threw his wet head toward his soaked back and exhaled. "Thank you."

Wallace didn't know if he'd done right to offer his spare room to the interim when there was a chance he'd be vacating to Sulphur Springs, but the Carlson's were in a bind of the best kind. Perhaps Pastor Carlson's wealthy brother-in-law would pay rent on his cousin's house when Wallace left.

"I never believed in love at first sight, Wallace." A picture of almost-five year-old Clara holding a pack of Lifesavers flashed before him. Wallace believed in it. At least in the birth of it as first sight. "But, having Maggie and Graham in the same house less than a day might prove me wrong."

Wallace hoped the relief he felt over Maggie's change of affection didn't show on his face. He attempted to cover it with a chuckle.

"Maybe Graham Campbell will prove to be just what the community needs. And you." He whistled. "And Maggie."

"Well, at least you don't need to feel awkward anymore." Wendell's smile was pastoral.

"Maggie is one of the kindest people I know. And a good friend."

"A friend indeed. I'm rather relieved for her sake that maybe she's…"

"Had a change of heart?"

"Yes."

Wendell shook Wallace's hand. "Ring the house when you return from your business trip, and we'll make arrangements." Wallace took a key from the hook near the door and handed it to Wendell. "Go 'head and move him in today. Here's the spare key."

When Wendell departed, Wallace slipped into his old room and changed into his suit. He paused at the mirror. "Should I shave off the beard?" No. With hat and umbrella in hand, he left the garage in his mechanic's care and began the drive to his potential future.

The heavy rains slowed his driving while adrenaline kept him shifting his position. Weary of thinking, he recited one of Clara's stories aloud, using the voices she would insert in her own telling. He sighed. The woman he loved had a way with words.

"What twenty-four-year old tells children's stories to himself." He laughed at the image of himself before slipping into the first verse of Amazing Grace in his own deep voice. Wallace leaned over the steering wheel and wiped the moisture from the windshield. Between the dip of the wipers, he managed to read the road sign. Almost there. He hushed and concentrated on the road. Ten miles later, Wallace drove past downtown Sulphur Springs and located Coomer's Garage.

The place had twice as many bays as Myers with a cement lot and autos lined up on the side of the building. Wallace blew out a breath and stepped onto the wet pavement and paced himself to the front door, glad the rain had subsided.

"I'm here to meet with Waylon Coomer."

Nineteen days ago he'd said goodbye to Clara Williams. Thirteen more were scheduled to pass before her return at the end of the month, the same ending that would close his life at Myers and begin his life in Sulphur Springs. The offer to manage the location was too good to ignore. He'd be able to provide a place for himself as well as the family he wouldn't have.

Clara. His heart twisted. Had she met with the publisher yet? "I'm praying for you, Little Butterfly." He couldn't recollect calling Clara by the pet name her Papa used, but the endearment reflected his feelings for her today. He hoped the publisher meeting transformed her into a confident writer.

His stomach set aside its nerves and summoned hunger. Wallace reckoned he should grab a late lunch before he drove back. He sat by himself in a diner booth and preferred to be eating Lena's meal he'd set aside yesterday. This meatloaf was dry. He pushed his plate aside then caught the eye of the lone man in the booth across from him. Wallace noticed him thumbing through a leather binder while he ate pie. The man nodded a greeting his way before turning the page.

"Would you like dessert?" Wallace grinned when the waitress raised her eyebrows at the discarded plate. "I suspect you're still hungry or maybe not hungry at all."

"I'll take coconut cream pie and coffee." The waitress turned and side stepped an approaching woman.

The man in the next booth spoke. "Lillian." A woman slid in next to him and weaved her arm through his just as he closed the binder. Wallace wished he were facing the other direction.

"It's been too long." The man kissed the woman on the cheek and then the lips. "The two weeks have dragged by, and I didn't like sleeping at the motel last night." He pulled a small gift box from his pants pocket and handed it to the her. "For you." The woman squealed. Wallace averted his eyes to the window, but was fully aware Lillian had received a necklace that earned the man another kiss.

The waitress returned with his dessert. "Do you have a newspaper here I could look through?" He needed a place for his eyes to settle. The waitress reached to the table behind his and produced a used copy. She moved to the booth and offered to take an order from the female newcomer, who only offered her thanks before dismissing the waitress.

"What is this?" Lillian pointed to the binder. Her deep voice grated on Wallace.

"It's someone's dream. A children's story."

"Yours?"

"Of course not. Let's get out of here."

Wallace glanced away from his paper to see them sliding from the booth. The man draped a camera bag around his neck. The lady picked up the binder.

"Why do you have this?"

"I took it. For spite. I'll burn it in your fireplace tonight to keep us warm." He kissed her lips. "Which is rather a shame because I like a good story."

Did they have no shame?

The lady giggled. "You're a despicable man, Andrew Slayton."

Impossible.

You won't believe what is sitting on my night stand. My lightning bug story, typed on fancy white paper and tied with Aunt Lena's drawings in a new leather binder. I wish you could see it.

Wallace's body tensed then flew into action. He yanked the man's arm to stop him.

141

"Give me that binder." He grabbed it from the woman. She screamed. The man pushed her out of the way then attempted to pull the binder free from Wallace, but Wallace slumped back onto the booth seat and pulled open the cover to reveal the first page.

"Clara." Wallace slammed the binder onto the table and stood. The man was taller than him, so Wallace's fist hit his lower jaw. He'd aimed for the man's nose, just below his wire-rimmed glasses. He'd never punched a grown man before. He'd never needed to.

Amid the chaos he heard a voice calling for the police. And a folded piece of tablet paper flashed across his mind.

Wallace pounded on the front door until someone opened it.

"Where's Ben? No one answered their door."

Lena gasped before pulling him inside. Henry sat in a chair with his torso slumped over his knees. He turned and glared.

"Where have you been? Your mechanic expected you back at four." His words were laced with anger. Wallace swallowed. Henry was not well. But Wallace shrugged away that thought. Someone more important was driving his actions.

"Where's Ben?" He reciprocated Henry's tone.

"He and Katherine dropped everything and headed to Austin. Garrett telephoned. Something happened with Clara." Lena's lip quivered. "Ben promised us she was okay, but we don't know what's wrong."

Wallace held up the binder and groaned. "I do."

Chapter 21

She wasn't dreaming. Real memories replayed themselves one after another. Andrew imposing himself, cheapening her first kiss. Assuming she'd join him in an encounter. He saw her as naive, easy prey. Uncle Joe's presence looming over her when Momma and Aunt Lena were away. As memories came to life, she realized Joe never harmed her. Taunting must have been his pleasure. He'd also seen her as naive, easy prey. Did Momma know? If Wallace knew she'd been preyed upon by two men, would he still want her?

Shame coursed through her. Clara tossed back covers and hastened to the bathroom where her stomach released its contents. Mary slipped in and wet a cloth. The cool moisture felt good against her forehead. They sat next to one another on the cold tile floor.

"Do you think you have a stomach virus?"

"A nervous stomach."

"Tomorrow's meeting?"

Tonight's memories.

"Must be." She despised lying.

Mary pulled her close. "Your stories are delightful and insightful."

Clara grasped the chance to divert her own mood. "Meeting a publisher is frightful." They giggled.

"You've already met him."

"No, I met a man who is head over heels for my friend."

Mary feigned fanning herself. "Who will surely be head over heels for your work. Porter has excellent taste." They giggled.

Clara stood and reached for her toothbrush. "I feel better and want to brush my teeth before I get back in bed."

As moments formed into the next hour, Clara once again found herself in the bathroom with Mary at her heels.

"Girls, are you alright?" Cass's voice sounded from the other side of the door. Mary glanced at Clara, who shook her head yes, before her friend explained what was wrong. Within moments, Cass was back with a bubbling Alka-Seltzer. Clara wrinkled her face and held her nose then guzzled the medicinal liquid. She was ready for a remedy. *If only it would remedy the memories.*

Clara slipped back into bed, but Mary didn't.

"Where's your binder?"

"In my drawer."

Clara watched Mary take hold of the book. "Follow me."

"What are we doing?" Clara threw back covers and stood, careful of her churning stomach lest the seltzer force its way up her throat. "You'll see." Mary clasped her hand and led Clara into the dining room before handing the binder to her. "Is it ready for your meeting?" Clara nodded. In fact, she'd neatly stuffed her handwritten pages in the back should Porter wish to see them.

Mary took back the binder. "We are banishing the binder from our room." She placed it reverently on the small chair by the dining room window. "You may wish it well or kiss it good-night. Then you cannot touch it until you leave for your meeting with Porter." Clara snickered. Dear Mary. Clueless this moment, but caring always.

The clock struck three. When Clara crawled under her covers, Mary slipped in beside her. The two of them talked. When thoughts of Maggie and of Porter turned to Andrew, Clara whimpered. She felt Mary turn on her side.

"Clara, has something happened between you and Andrew that is bothering you?"

"Yes. I'm not interested in him anymore. He got kinda mad about that."

"He'll just have to get over it."

Clara exhaled. "Mary, he thinks I misled him. Maybe he's right. Maybe I should be ashamed of my actions with him."

"I don't think so. You are unattached and he, or maybe the life he represents, made you curious. Maybe that's how he feels about you too."

"I'm not unattached. My heart belongs to Wallace, if he still wants it."

"Of course he does."

Clara told the tale of the telephone calls while sleep began to take over.

144

While the Rain Whispered

Morning brought with it a light breakfast for Clara, then she and Mary whiled away the Tuesday in their room separated from Andrew. Clara felt a tinge of guilt when Cass let on to the household that she was recovering from a sick stomach. However, Cass's soft smiles at Clara hinted she was aware of her heart's condition. Close to noon, Abigail Forder slipped into the room and sat beside Clara on the bed. Mary joined them.

"Andrew is leaving to do a lunch errand." She ran a hand over Clara's hair. "Come out of hiding and get dressed. I've got my own errands to run and you girls are coming with me."

Clara bit her lip.

"Don't fret," Mrs. Forder patted her hand, "his last session will end before we get back."

Mary's voice was coaxing. "You'll have to face him someday, but not today. Feel like getting out?"

Clara hugged Mrs. Forder. "Yes."

Within ten minutes Garrett was home for the day and released the car to his mother. Within ten more minutes, the trio walked into Kruger's Jewelers. *I can't believe it.* Clara thought she'd grown accustomed to shopping with the Forders, but these glittering displays begging for her gaze made her mouth drop.

Mrs. Forder spoke as she walked through the door. "I have a special order to pick up. You girls shop around." Shop around? Clara grinned. She'd limit herself to looking around and try not to gawk. Mary tugged on her arm. "Let's go look at engagement rings." Clara rolled her eyes. "Oh, yes, let's."

"Andrew?"

Mrs. Forder's voice announced the name. Clara turned to her right and felt her knees go weak. She supported herself against a glass case. Andrew was face to face with Mrs. Forder. He wiggled a small box in the air. "My errand. Bye now." Mary placed her arm around Clara's waist as Andrew scampered toward the front door next to where they stood. Mrs. Forder pursued him.

He paused then leaned into Clara's ear. "Don't look so repulsed. This isn't for you, pet." Clara felt Mary's grip tighten. His eyes met Clara's then he spoke as though addressing a crowd. "Good luck with the publisher." Andrew let the door slam behind him.

"He had the audacity to buy you a gift? And whisper in your ear?" Mary's huff was warm on Clara's neck.

"No. He said the gift wasn't for me."

Mary twirled Clara to face her. "Good. But who's it for?"

"He didn't say and I don't care."

Clara assured Mrs. Forder she was fine. In fact, she was very fine since the gift wasn't for her. Thinking Andrew wanted to lure her with jewelry had disgusted her.

Lunch and a stop at the salon for manicures filled the afternoon. Clara again found herself standing over a glass counter. Salesman in suits boasting displays of glittering diamonds were replaced by bottles of shiny colors and a lady attendant dressed in a pale pink uniform. Mary pointed to a bottle titled Apple Red. "Enjoy Clara. None of us pamper ourselves much with manicures back in Layton." Some of us never do. Clara selected Soft Peach, a pale, warm coral to compliment the burnt orange dress she'd wear tomorrow.

One awkward encounter with Andrew did not lead to another, for as promised, he was gone when the ladies returned. Despite seeing him in a most unpredictable circumstance, Clara had enjoyed her afternoon and evening. The shame she felt had been silenced by anticipation to meet with Porter. And nerves. And, she'd be out the door in the morning before Andrew was due to arrive.

She sighed and sipped the cocoa Cass had prepared, though she was already full from supper. The four women sat cuddled on the couch in the Forder's front room. The hour was early, yet Garrett had dosed in the living room chair with Madie asleep in his lap. Clara was tired and didn't want to follow Garrett's example. She preferred to crawl in bed and fall asleep. She stood from the couch and excused herself, but Mary refrained her.

"We'll go with you." The other women stood. Clara had intended to grab her binder from the dining room, but the entourage guided her steps to the bedroom. No matter, she could make a ceremony of picking up the binder in the morning. She smiled at the memory of Mary's proclamation the night before.

Clara noted that Mrs. Forder slipped to her room and then quickly returned as Cass and Mary kept her occupied laying out her outfit for tomorrow's meeting. "Clara. For you." Mrs. Forder handed her a small, square box labeled Krugers with a green ribbon tied around it. Clara's hands trembled as she took it. Once again her capacity to receive without giving back in near portion felt full. But, all eyes were on her and each face held a wide grin.

She unwrapped the box to find a bracelet with pale blue rhinestones set in gold filigree. Tears welled unbeckoned. Mary took it from her. "It's in honor of your meeting tomorrow." Goodness. However they dressed her up, Clara feared she was just a simple writer of a simple children's stories. These fine folks might be disappointed with tomorrow's outcome. Mary clasped the bracelet on her wrist. "It's from your Momma and Papa, and Lena and Henry."

Her lips quivered. Clara couldn't bear the love and the sacrifice this represented. "It's their way of being here." Mary held out Clara's arm to show off the piece. "It's beautiful." Clara tasted salty tears as she spoke. "Whew," Mrs. Forder declared, "I'm glad you like it. They trusted me with picking something for you." Clara turned to Mrs. Forder. "It's perfect." Cass brought over the burnt orange dress. "These are beautiful with each other."

Beautiful with each other.

Clara grasped the words and held them near her heart for they captured how she felt about the Forders and her family. And Wallace. God had graced her with them.

----------◆•◆•◆----------

Clara knew this Wednesday morning would remain with her until her mind grew weary of holding memories. This was the morning for which she had risked her future with Wallace. This was the morning she would rely on the reputation and abilities of no one other than Clara Williams. She would offer Porter Franklin her vulnerability bound in leather.

The girl staring in the bedroom mirror faded into the woman staring back at her. Clara felt confident. Her burnt orange and cream dress suited her figure and hair color. Her hair—she hadn't yet grown used to seeing her slender neck exposed, full, russet curves rather than waves. The short style suited the confident young woman she wanted to be this morning. The love of family adorned her wrist. She felt embraced by the love of Wallace who'd released her to this very day. She'd prayed. She was ready.

Mary walked in from the bathroom.

"You look perfect, Clara."

"Thank you."

Behind her, Mrs. Forder stopped in the hallway and glanced into the room. "Ready?" Clara nodded yes and followed them into the dining room to bid Cass and Madie good-bye. Garrett rose from his seat at the table as they approached.

"Oh, Clara, you look like a real author. Well, I've never met one before. But I think so anyway." Clara chuckled at Madie's compliment. The young girl set down her glass of juice and pushed her chair back from the table. Small hands clasped Clara's. "And you're so pretty too."

"Good luck, Clara. I'll be praying." Cass smiled.

"Thank you both."

Garrett urged them on. "Time to go."

Clara walked to the chair beside the dining room window and gasped. The binder was not where she and Mary had left it. Her stomach knotted as her eyes darted to Mary, then the table, then swept the room. The binder was nowhere to be seen.

"Did someone move the binder?" She worked to control panic and accusation in her voice.

"Remember, Mr. Slayton took it." Madie pronounced.

Gasps filled the air.

"Mr. Slayton?" Clara's throat ached controlling a sob.

Tears came to Madie's eyes. "He said he was taking it to Mr. Franklin for you. So he'd have lots of time to see it."

Clara's felt the room spin. Mary took hold of her hand.

Mrs. Forder spoke up. "Madie, when did he take it?"

"Yesterday when he finished teaching me. What's wrong?"

Garrett bent before his daughter. "Clara didn't know he was taking it, so she's surprised."

"He said she asked him to. I believed him." Madie's lip quivered. Clara touched Madie's cheek. "You should have believed him. You didn't do anything wrong."

Garrett rose. "Let's get you to that appointment. Why Andrew took the binder, I don't know, but at least it's at the publisher's office."

No, I feel certain it isn't. Clara exhaled. "Let's go."

———————•◦◆◦•———————

Andrew's behavior set the mood for a ride peppered with frail assurances and awkward silence. Sorting her thoughts, Clara twirled the bracelet round and round her wrist. She couldn't tell the others that Andrew took the binder for spite, though she felt he had. If indeed he'd given it to Porter, then Clara suspected he was enjoying the thought of her displeasure and confusion. She brushed those thoughts away to ponder what solutions she could offer Porter to get her work in front of him.

Flanked by three Forders, Clara felt relieved to enter Porterhouse Publishers. The scents of ink and paper soothed her nerves. The clatter of typewriters bid her hello. She definitely wanted to learn typing. The front room was lined with desks, many burdened with stacks of bound papers. Manuscripts?

Her hands felt despairingly empty. What havoc had Andrew brought upon her. *Dear God, help me.*

"May I help you?" Clara smiled at the lady seated at the front desk. "I have an appointment with Mr. Porter Franklin." Garrett tapped her elbow then nodded to the back of the room. Porter was making his way to them. "He sees us."

"Good morning, everyone." Though professional in tone, Clara noted his gaze linger on Mary and offer the smile of a man, not a publisher. "Clara, my office is in the back." He looked at the three Forders and pointed to chairs. "You all can sit over here. Our receptionist can get you coffee." He glanced at Clara's hands, but then nodded toward the back. She followed him and sat in the leather chair facing a large cherry wood desk. Shelves of books, pictures, and knick knacks lined the painted walls. The office smelled of his cologne. Porter sat in the leather chair behind his desk. A clock ticked a reminder that time never stops.

"Thank you for meeting with me." Clara cleared her throat.

"Tell me a bit about your stories." He hadn't seen for himself? Of course not.

Her thoughts tangled. "They are children's stories based on insects. Each one teaches a value. My aunt draws the illustrations." Say more. Her passion stepped in and took over the conversation. At last, Porter grinned.

"Have you titled them?"

She felt her cheeks heat. "Windy Hop Tales."

His eyes lit up, and he smiled.

"Your aunt is an artist?"

"She can draw."

The side of his mouth lifted.

"In the business, if I like the illustrations, I'll use them. If not, I'll use an in-house artist."

Clara nodded. What if they liked her stories but not Aunt Lena's pictures? She swallowed. Or the other way around. Would they use Lena's pictures for another writer?

"Can I see the sample you brought?" The room spun.

"Don't you have it, Porter?" She knew he didn't.

His eyebrows rose, and he tapped a pen on his desk. "No, why would I?"

Clara chose to be a young woman and not throw a fit. "Of course you wouldn't. It's exactly what I feared."

"Clara. I'm confused. Did you bring the story?"

"No. I don't have it. Andrew took it."

Porter rose from his chair and came to sit in the chair opposite hers. He remained silent while they stared eye to eye. Clara exhaled then retold the events of the morning.

"Why would Andrew do that?"

Clara lowered her head. "Revenge."

She leaned toward him. "I've wasted your time. And I desperately need to talk to Mrs. Forder and Mary." She released tears to roll down her checks. "We'll talk more about your stories later, but something is wrong. I'll send Mrs. Forder and Mary to you."

Porter walked away, and a moment later Mrs. Forder and Mary walked in.

An hour after that, Garrett Forder telephoned Ben Williams. Clara was going home.

Chapter 22

The house didn't smell of his after shave because Andrew hadn't been there. "He never came." Cass sat in the large chair next to Garrett in the front room and relayed the morning she and Madie had. Clara pulled the blanket tighter around her and snuggled closer to Mrs. Forder on the couch while Mary pressed next to her and rubbed her short bob. Madie had been sent next door to get her out of the house, free from conversation about her tutor.

How dare Andrew use the innocent girl in his scheme.

"When he didn't show up, and we didn't get a telephone call from him, I knew he must be up to no good. I had to tell Madie that Mr. Slayton probably did something wrong, and was ashamed." Her hands covered her cheeks. "Clara, I had no idea he'd been so cruel to you. The man tutored Madie in my presence every day, and I didn't suspect a thing." Her voice rose. "I put you and my daughter in harm's way. We let him escort you. Oh, my." Clara didn't want Cass to feel responsible in any way. "He fooled all of us. He made sure nothing he did around Madie or all of us together cast any doubt on him."

Indeed, the Forders had become family to her in the two weeks she'd lived here. Did they know how much their gift of time and home meant to her? Andrew could not tarnish that. These folks were hurting on her behalf and carrying a burden of responsibility she wished they wouldn't bear.

"I have come to love all of you like family. You have given me opportunities I would never imagine. None of us should let Andrew ruin that." Clara sat up. "Look at me. I'm fine. And I can write more stories. If they are supposed to be printed, they will be. I suspect there will be some pretty tight connections with a publisher." Mary laughed.

Momma and Papa were due to arrive around nine o'clock. Poor Momma. She didn't like traveling, much less a four to five hour trip.

"Who else at home knows about the mess, Mrs. Forder?" Wallace?

"I'm not certain."

Cass rose when someone knocked, then opened the door to Porter. When

151

Mary turned to face him, Clara released the blanket revealing a wrinkled orange and cream dress.

"Sit here." Cass pointed to her chair, then went and sat next to Mrs. Forder.

Mary smiled. "Did you find him?"

Porter grunted. "I rode to the typical places I thought I might see Andrew, even spoke to his father. No one I talked to has seen him."

"Maybe he's in the typical places you'd never go to." The words blurted from her lips, and Clara blushed.

Clara knew that once Mrs. Forder had informed Garrett of Andrew's behavior, he'd used Porter's phone to call Papa and sent Porter here to check on Cass and Madie. All trust in Andrew had died. When Garrett returned home, Porter had left to try to find the man and confront him.

Cibby brought Madie back, loaded with a strawberry cake. "Miss Clara, I do hope to see you again someday." Cibby placed a pouch in her hand. Clara's nose knew what was inside. "Your special potpourri." She sniffed the pouch. "I love the smell. Thank you. It will remind me of here."

The group nibbled on a light meal and dessert, then Porter began to bid his farewells. He drew Clara to the front room within earshot of the others.

"We will meet again about your stories."

"I can rewrite that story. I have it right here." She patted her heart.

"No, Clara. You won't love it like you once did." He put his hands on both her shoulders. "Go home. Write a new story then send me all the ones you have. And Clara, after that, dig deep and write your own story. The tale of your joys, struggles, and love. What you've learned right here." He pointed toward her heart.

He stepped back and called for Mary. "Clara, I hope to see you again much sooner than later." He winked at Mary. "Safe travels." Her friend walked him to the front porch, and Clara returned to the others.

She opened the front door. No words, no gasps. Only touch. Clara wrapped her arms around home. Momma smelled of lavender. Papa's smell was more natural, comprised of worry and haste, but Clara let it fill her. Another day he'd smell of woods and spice.

Wallace had not come.

Momma leaned back from their embrace. Her silent question obvious. "I'm alright. He didn't harm me in any way." Momma's tears rolled over smiling lips, and her hand moved to touch her short hair. "My sassy Clara. The style suits you."

Papa kissed her cheek. "Hello my Little Butterfly." Clara hated the turmoil she read on his face.

"I'm sorry I caused you so much worry."

His hand stroked her back. "With great love comes great concern. You can't have one without the other."

"Come inside. It's misty out here." Clara grabbed a hand of each and pulled them into the house. Tension hung in the air.

"Katherine." Mrs. Forder was at Momma's side in two steps.

"Abigail. I've missed you." The two hugged. "How are you holding up with Mason gone?"

"The folks in this room have kept me content and busy, but I keep walking around the deep hole of Mason's absence." The two embraced again.

"Your Clara," Abigail Forder's words were lost in emotion.

"My Clara is fine. She assures us. And looking quite charming." Clara smiled, but wondered if Momma missed the long locks she'd sported for almost ten years.

Garrett had risen to address Papa. "Ben." Papa put him at ease. "Clara seems good. Thank you for telephoning us, Garrett."

After a shuffle of motion and tangled conversation of who back home knew what, and what did folks here know, the Forders dismissed themselves. Clara found herself alone on the couch with her parents. A tray of sandwiches and cake remained untouched while the tale of Andrew was told. Momma took her arm and fingered the new bracelet as she listened. When their questions settled, Clara took a bite of sandwich and asked about the unexplained matter nagging at her.

"Papa, why didn't you tell Wallace you were coming here?"

"I didn't see him. His car wasn't at the garage when I drove by to tell Henry we were leaving. I'm sure Henry filled him in later." He pulled her to him.

"We'll telephone the store in the morning and talk to Henry. He can put the others at ease."

"Will he tell Wallace?"

"Butterfly, we'll make sure Wallace knows you're safe."

"I miss him."

Papa's lips lifted on one side. Clara knew he was suppressing a told-you-so smile. Momma made no attempt to hide her grin. "I think he misses you too." A look passed between her parents. She knew them well—they were withholding information.

"I saw that look."

Papa laughed. "I hope he recognizes you." Clara knew he was diverting.

"Momma? What was that look?"

"Goodness, Clara." She paused. "I wonder what he'll think about your hair."

"I think he'll like it." I hope he does.

Clara clasped a hand of each. She was convinced the look between them was about more than her hair, but she's also knew her parents were tired and drained of emotion. She'd trust them to tell her in time what they held between them. Besides, she still had a heavy matter to bring up.

"Momma, can we all talk about Uncle Joe?"

She felt Momma twitch.

"Why, Little Butterfly?" Papa's fingers tightened around her hand.

"Because I've had some memories."

Momma whimpered, but shook her head up and down.

———— ◆ ————

The scent of bacon roused Clara. Rain tapped against the house and invited her to stay snuggled in covers. A glance at the clock showed it was eight in the morning. Thursday morning, the day she might have known if the publisher was interested in her stories. Instead, it was the day Momma and Papa were here to take her home, and she was no closer to being published than the day she left Layton. Careful not to disturb Mary sleeping next to her, Clara sat up enough to see Mrs. Forder, who'd given up her room to Momma and Papa, was no longer in bed beside Madie.

Clara lay still and glanced around the bedroom, noting unfinished library books, photographs—she shuddered—postcards, purses, a perfume bottle, jewelry, and the empty place where her binder had been. All tokens of an ending adventure

Her mind drifted to Wallace. Had he slept, not knowing how she fared? Would he have come if given the chance? Yes, because he has a way of being where she needs him.

The memory of last night's talk stirred, making peace and sadness swirl inside her. How proud to know Momma had stood up for her to Uncle Joe. Her memories had spoken truth. Joe had taunted her, but he had not tainted her. She sighed. Joe had harmed Aunt Lena, but Henry came along and became her balm. Clara grinned, remembering when her aunt and uncle met then fell in love.

Papa cried last night. "Not being there for you, Momma, and Lena in the years Joe threatened your home is my second greatest regret."

Papa entered her life when she was five years old, he and Momma having lived apart that entire time. Although they had unknowingly pined for one another, misunderstandings had stretched their time apart into five years. Clara had known nothing more than that for it was a story left untold.

As he'd wept, Momma had intertwined her fingers with his across Clara's lap. "The reason behind not being there is my greatest regret," he'd added. Clara had looked him in the eye, "What was the reason, Papa?" She'd regretted the question the moment she asked it, for the shame on Papa's face said more than she wanted to know. "I was human. Never leave your strengths unguarded." Momma had kissed his hand.

And as it had been all her life, the tale of their separation remained untold. The time may never come for its full telling. Clara didn't need to hear the story. She already knew the happy ending.

"Rise and shine, ladies." The door came ajar to reveal Mrs. Forder. "Breakfast in ten minutes." Mary roused beside her. "I'm going to miss you." Her voice was raspy. "Me too." Madie spoke as she bounded on top of them.

Clara lifted the covers to allow Madie a place between them. "Aunt Mary will have Mr. Franklin on her mind. And you have more pictures to draw in your book."

Mary spoke through a yawn. "I dreamed about Porter."

"I dreamed my new tutor was an old lady with warts. Eww." Madie giggled.

"I'll miss you both too."

Mary sat up. "Time to dress. I'm hungry."

Within minutes, Clara walked into the front room, delighted at the sight of Momma setting biscuits on the table and Papa sipping coffee in a front room chair.

"Morning, Little Butterfly." Clara bent and hugged him. "Morning Papa." He smelled of spice and woods.

She moved to the dining room and kissed Momma. "Morning."

"Good morning Clara. Did you sleep?"

"Yessum. Did you?"

"Yes. And I only woke at the smell of coffee. Cass and Abigail cooked all this." As far back as Clara could recall, Momma had dubbed Abigail her most unlikely friend.

"Garrett talked me into driving only half-way today. Your Momma is getting her adventure."

"Really?"

"We're going to see the Capitol and leave after lunch." Momma's voice carried a lilt. "The light rain won't spoil my adventure."

Clara's mouth fell open. Then dread hit her at the thought of bumping into Andrew followed by disappointment that home was another day away. Yet, her parents deserved a little adventure of their own.

Clara sat down at the breakfast table and recounted items Momma might enjoy viewing in the Capitol. The conversation gathered participants so that an air of excitement over must-sees and remember-thats settled in the room.

"The rotunda is flanked by ornate staircases…"

A ringing telephone interrupted Garrett's explanation of the Capitol. He moved to answer it.

156

"Henry." Clara jerked her eyes to Papa at the mention of the name. Papa's eyes were wide.

"Sure. He's right here."

Clara's heart beat faster when Garrett motioned Papa to the telephone. She reckoned Uncle Henry was impatient for news of her welfare. Maybe Wallace was too and was hovering over him by the telephone. Conversation hushed when Papa talked.

"Yes. She's good. Just a bit shaken up. The short version of what happened is the tutor stole her story binder." Papa's mouth dropped, and he eyed Momma with a wrinkled brow. "How do you know what happened?"

"What!" Clara jumped up, knocking her chair to the floor. With two wide steps she stood before Papa. "What? What?" Papa shook his hand in her face, and Clara stopped. Her stomach knotted and her breaths increased. She paced in a circle forcing her curiosity to be quiet and not blurt questions. Momma grabbed her hands to still her, but Clara pulled loose and kept in motion. Papa's whys, and hows, and whens mocked her angst.

Then Papa pressed a hand against the wall as though he needed its support. "Wallace was handcuffed?"

A mutual gasp thundered through the house. Momma plopped on the couch. Not one person remained at the table. Clara pulled at her hair and began to cry before dropping next to Momma. Her body swayed back and forth with anxiety. She knew folks were mumbling their questions and disbeliefs, but blood pounding in her ears muffled the voices. Her eye caught Cass leading Madie toward the bedrooms. Mary sat at her feet postured to comfort.

"Alright, Henry. We'll be home around lunch tomorrow. I got to hang up and explain things or this house is gonna blow up with tension."

At last.

Papa hung up the telephone, then looked Clara in the eyes. "Wallace is fine." She watched his uneven gait bring him to her as Mary moved. He sat beside her, and Clara gripped his hand. Papa lowered his head and blew out a breath then addressed her.

"Clara, Mr. Myers has to sell the garage or he'll go bankrupt." Her chin quivered. "Wallace doesn't have the funds to buy it." She recalled the look between her parents last night. This news had to be the reason.

"What will he do?" The words escaped through whimpers.

"That's where Henry's news comes in. Try and hear me out." He addressed the rest of the room.

"Wallace went to Sulphur Springs yesterday for a job interview and ate lunch at a diner. A young man in the next booth was met by a woman. The man was Andrew Slayton."

Clara squeezed her eyes shut. Papa's words made her head throb. A collision between the man who loved her and the man who mocked her— miles from their homes—was unbelievable. She uttered her question. "How did Wallace know it was him?"

Papa told a tale of the binder in Andrew's possession as an act of revenge, an amorous rendezvous between a man and woman, and a jewelry gift. The pieces between here and there began to fit together.

He continued on. Her Wallace had been heroic.

"So, when Wallace punched Andrew, he staggered, but threw a punch back. Someone called the police. Then Wallace grabbed him into a choke hold. Andrew suddenly relaxed and said he didn't want any more trouble. He was wrong to take the binder. Keep it. Wallace was a lucky man, all that stuff, as though he were repentant. Wallace released him and about that time the police showed up. Wallace reckoned they were nearby because they were quick to get there. Both men were handcuffed and taken to the police station."

If silence could speak, it would be shouting.

The tale took a turn, and Papa shared how Andrew wasn't repentant at all. He'd been trying to avoid an encounter with the police. In fact, the police department had an eye on Andrew and the lady.

"Andrew made money betting on horses. He and Lillian, the woman, met at Epsom Downs in Houston and were regulars at Alamo Downs." Papa raised his eyebrows at Garrett. "When pari-mutuel betting was rescinded by the state legislature in May, Andrew and Lillian started running numbers from her house in Sulphur Springs."

"Running numbers?"

"Illegal betting, Clara."

Garrett whistled. "A criminal in my own home. Tutoring my daughter. I must be a fool not to pick up on it."

"No. You've only been here two weeks since all this started. Reckon his father knows?"

"I hope not, but greed has lots of friends." He cleared his throat. "The authorities could ask the same about me. I need to tell the Governor what I know and didn't know." He grinned. "They must not be good at what they did, to be caught so soon."

"Papa, what about Wallace?"

He smiled. "Police believed the truth. He was a man in love looking for a job at the right place and the right time. He wasn't charged, got released, drove home, and knocked on Henry's door late last night."

Clara felt her cheeks heat as emotion rushed through her. She was a woman in love, in the wrong place at the wrong time. She and Wallace needed each other. Her eyes glanced at Momma. "Papa, can we go home today?"

"I think that's a good idea."

Chapter 23

Clara rested her head against the window and listened as rain pattered against it. Papa wiped the windshield repeatedly with his handkerchief. She sat enclosed with Momma and Papa in their auto, and what could have felt claustrophobic was cozy. Her world at this moment was small, and she was content in it.

Her traveling adventure had ended. She hoped that one day her mind would weed out the bad memories and relish the sights and opportunities the Forders had made possible. She'd packed a few photographs Andrew had taken. She and Mary at the Alamo. She, Mary, Cass, and Madie at Barton Springs. The only one of Mary and Porter that her friend would relinquish. Mary's smile had missed the click, so the photograph didn't display her joy. Porter's joy, however, shown all over his face. In time, she might share them with Wallace. "I'll keep the others. You can see them whenever you like, except these," Mary had declared as she tore up any photographs with Andrew in them.

How strange that the binder Andrew had compiled now rested in Wallace's care. She reckoned she would discard it. Porter speculated wisely. Her lightning bug story now struck her as tarnished. "Perhaps another lightning bug will light upon me and reveal a new tale." She grinned at her pun.

Porter told her to write from her heart. Images of she and Wallace, Momma and Papa, her brothers, family, and friends danced before her. What tales would they tell in the pages of her story? Life is filled with stories. One just has to look for them. Hum. Perhaps those lines would open her book.

Truth was, Wallace had reminded her of something similar months ago. *"Clara, if you want to know people, look at their eyes. Their stories are shadowed behind them."* She wondered if that was the moment she'd fallen in love with him. Perhaps for some, love reveals itself in an eye-catching moment. For others, like her, love reveals itself through many unnoticed moments.

"Do y'all think Wallace will move?"

Momma turned in her seat and faced Clara. "He's already moved into that small house his cousin owns."

She leaned forward in surprise. "He has?" Momma shook her head up and down. "On Saturday."

Clara realized that's why he didn't answer when she telephoned.

"Then why go talk to someone about a job in Sulphur Springs?"

Papa's voice was matter of fact. "I reckon he'll go wherever a job takes him."

"And leave Layton? Isn't there something else he could do?"

"I don't know, Little Butterfly. But I suspect he's considered all his options."

Clara would do the same and knew only one option existed. To go wherever Wallace went, even if it meant leaving Layton. She had the rest of the ride home to absorb that truth.

Early afternoon Papa stopped at a diner miles beyond Waco while the rain ceased. Momma knelt behind his open door and rubbed his bum leg until he felt he could stand on it. She pulled him from the seat, and together they walked inside the diner. Clara wished she or Momma knew how to drive and could relieve him.

A newspaper lay in the chair that Clara pulled out around the square table. Two photographs under a headline caught her eye. A woman she didn't know. And Andrew. "Illegal betting ring busted in Sulphur Springs."

"What did you just say?"

"I read a headline. Look, Papa." She handed the paper to him. Momma leaned over his shoulder. "So there's the filthy, rotten culprit." The paper wrinkled against Papa's tightening grip and his face turned red. "To think that man had his hands on my daughter."

Clara's stomach knotted, and she moved to kneel at his chair. "Papa, he didn't harm me. I'm fine. Your anger means the world to me, but you can let it go. I want to move on. I want us all to move on. Justice will be served to Andrew." He rubbed her head. "You're right. Vengeance belongs to God." He tossed the paper to the next table, and they settled in to look at menus.

"Did you see his glasses were cracked?" Momma looked over her menu and bit her lip. Papa didn't look up, but took hold of Momma's humor. "I reckon Wallace did a job on him. And, that Lillian is right ugly if you ask me." Clara laughed until the pain eased. She'd been wrong back in Austin. A little curiosity can be harmful.

Somewhere between the first and last bite of her grilled cheese, Clara felt Momma's gentle kick against her shin. "I do have one bit of news." Clara smiled at the sheepish look on her mother's face. "What is it?" She felt her eyes shift over to Papa and caught his wink at Momma. "I asked your Papa to get us a telephone." In one motion Clara was scooted from the table and on her feet. "Stop the world. Momma wants a telephone." She moved to hug her. Both parents laughed. "Yes, with you bein' gone," Papa explained with amusement, "Katherine Williams determined that those she loves may not always be in walkin' distance." A warmth came over Clara. Sweet Momma. Family truly was her life's adventure. Clara reckoned she must have always fancied the same for her daughter. Perhaps not her child's only adventure, but her dearest one. Clara sighed, knowing she now perceived what Momma had always known.

The sun had begun to set when Papa pulled in front of Aunt Lena's house. It was odd not seeing Wallace's Plymouth parked outside the garage when they passed. She'd be there tomorrow before he opened shop.

Jacob sat on the front step playing his harmonica and came running when he spied them. "Clara!" His embrace was strong as he lifted her from the auto and swung her in a circle. She clung to his neck, laughing and crying at the same time. A light mist hit her skin. Would she never be free of rain? Papa beeped the horn, and Jacob hollered for the others. Family paraded out the front door, and when Clara got to the porch, she was tangled in the arms of welcome home.

Lena squealed. "Your hair is divine." As though no one had noticed until that moment, variations of approval and bewilderment were expressed. Uncle Henry pulled her to him. "Why, you look like the little Clara I met at the boarding house. All spunk and sass." He pulled her tight, but not before she noticed the dark circles under his eyes. She felt his heart beat and spoke against his chest. "Thank you, Uncle Henry. I think." He patted her back and whispered, "I couldn't lose another little girl, even it was just to the big city." He released her. Clara glanced at Papa, whose quick nod affirmed her suspicion. Uncle Henry was struggling in his dark place. Her chest tightened. She wished she'd been here for him. She was now.

"Well, come in out of the rain. I just pulled cornbread from the oven to go with our vegetable soup." Clara almost mentioned the lasagna she'd tried in Austin, but thought better of it, wondering if she would ever swallow a bite of it again, for she couldn't stomach the memory of that meal. Lena spread her arms wide, "Find a seat anywhere." She winked at Clara. "Save a place for one more. He'll be here anytime."

It was her.

He could see Clara, illuminated by his headlights, shadowed behind gentle rain, waving at him from Henry's porch. He lifted his tall body from inside the auto and advanced toward her. Every fiber longed to pull her body against his. She met him at the top step.

"I'm home." Her thin fingers touched his face. "You grew a beard."

"I needed to forget what was between us." One side of his mouth lifted. "I didn't."

He placed his fingers beneath her locks and rubbed soft tendrils between his fingers. "You cut your hair."

"I needed to remember what was between us." She spread a slow deliberate smile. "I did."

Doubt fled and reason followed. His will surrendered.

Wallace pulled her body against his, securing her with an arm around her back and a hand against her seductive short locks. He groaned at the feel of her curves and softness against his frame. His lips brushed the angel kiss on her cheek, then with faltering restraint he bent and kissed her lips, knowing the delight would make him want all of her.

And he *would* have all of her. In time.

Wallace James would marry this girl and live life with her, even if it meant making their home in his boyhood room at Ma and Pa's.

He felt her relax against him, then move her hands to pull his face closer. Her lips moved with his own until he felt her speak against his mouth. "I love you." Between kisses he spoke "I. Love. You. Too."

She broke free and stared at him. Her eyes pleading for his proposal. He knew her well enough to see that.

"I'm moving to Sulphur Springs."

"I know. So am I. With you."

He kissed the top of her head and laughed.

"Marry me, Wallace, and make me your wife."

That was all he'd wanted for as long as he could remember.

"Why, you're sure full of sass. But I reckon I could put up with that." He dropped to one knee. "I'll marry you Clara, if you'll have me. Will you?"

She removed his watch and placed it in his pants pocket. His body trembled with her nearness. "Yes, for as long as we both shall live."

Chapter 24

It seemed that a lifetime had passed since the last family dinner in this room. Clara sat a white plate on the table then placed a knife and fork beside it. The sound of Momma and Aunt Lena chattering in the kitchen drifted into the dining room. Uncle Henry, Papa, Jacob, and Wallace played gin rummy around the card table in the front room while the younger ones set Monopoly in the boy's bedroom. Pa and Ma James and various James siblings would soon arrive. The house would be pregnant with people.

Clara sighed as contentment swept through her. These people were her adventure. They were the gifts God had given her to treasure. He'd been gracious to her. Not that the world wasn't full of sights she'd love to visit, but among these folks is where she would dwell. And any future children God gave to her and Wallace. Her cheeks heated at the thought.

"Clara." Momma called from the kitchen. Lena's giggle mingled with her words. "Set another place. We have a friend coming." Clara chuckled. At this rate, she'd have to sit in Wallace's lap at the table.

As if on cue, the man walked into the dining room and placed a quiet kiss on her lips. His chin, freed of whiskers, was rugged against her own. In two days, he'd become adept at sneaking kisses during brief moments alone. Her body responded. "Eight weeks." His whispered words were warm in her ears. She would become his wife the first Saturday in December. Yes, they must endure some weeks apart as he began his job in Sulphur Springs, but Clara would occupy the lonely hours with planning a wedding and writing another child's story. Wallace moved toward the kitchen. "I'm thirsty." He winked then moved into the kitchen. Unless someone joined her in the dining room, she'd receive another kiss as he passed back through. She took another plate from the sideboard.

Yesterday Wallace had expressed concern over taking her to Sulphur Springs where any remnants of Andrew may linger. After all, the wrongdoer had spent days and nights there.

"I can't take you there, Clara."

Panic made her queasy.

"Yes, you can. You will."

"I'll find other work."

"No, you won't."

"You're right."

"Of course I am." She hugged him. "My place is with you. The address doesn't matter." Although she'd miss Momma and Papa. But she could ring them now.

And yesterday, Wallace had made a confession.

"I need to tell you something you won't like hearing."

She was quite over hearing news she wouldn't like, but smiled. "What it is?"

He'd pulled a faded piece of paper with worn edges from his pocket and handed it to her. She unfolded it and felt her jaw drop.

"Where did you find this?"

"Outside the community center five years ago." He lowered his head, but she lifted his chin.

"You've had it all this time?"

"Yes. I wasn't truthful with you that night. I didn't lie, but I didn't tell the truth either. I found it and just wanted to have a piece of you with me."

She giggled.

"It's not funny. I felt bad about it all these years. Will you forgive me and can you trust me?"

She touched his cheek. "Yes and yes. It's kinda sweet." She bit her lip and raised her eyebrows. "Is there anything else you need to tell me?"

He winked and pulled her close. "Only one more truth I've kept secret." She tensed, and his lips brushed her hair. "I loved you long before I should have." She squeezed him. "You're a good man."

Wallace passed back through the dining room, his hands loaded with a platter of fried chicken. Aunt Lena and Momma paraded behind him holding bowls of mashed potatoes, green beans, and gravy. Her stomach growled. A kiss would have to wait, but hunger of another sort would soon be filled.

A knock at the front door grabbed her attention. "Pony, good to see you."

She overheard Papa welcoming Wallace's family. Clara sucked in a breath as she moved to greet the Jameses. She'd been around Pa and Ma James plenty at church, tent revivals, and church socials, but this would be her first time to linger with them as family. Did they think her good enough for their fine son?

"Clara." Ella James, Ma, grabbed her in a tight hug. "At last. I've known for years you were the woman for our Wallace." Her short, broad body felt odd in Clara's arms. She smiled, knowing she'd soon get used to the feel of her. "Thank you. I love him." Ma James stepped back, but kept her arms on Clara's shoulders. Wallace came to stand beside his mother. "He was a bear while you were gone." Wallace laughed. Ma James touched her short locks. "I like your haircut."

Other greetings, hugs, and congratulations ended, and folks began to find their seating for the meal when Papa opened the door to Garrett Forder. Something was up, for Papa's smile was wide to the point of looking unnatural. Others stared in confusion. Did he feel like a spectacle?

Clara's being felt off center as emotions from Austin collided with those from home. She felt herself at the Forder table, in the bedroom with Mary, and on the streets of the city as much as she felt herself standing in Momma's front room with Wallace beside her.

"Garrett, is everyone back home?" She felt Wallace's fingers brush her back as though he were steadying her.

"No, Clara. I came for unexpected business. I'll be going back tomorrow." His eyes roamed the room as though they didn't know where to rest. Pity awakened in Clara. Was this eloquent man struggling to face once again those who loved her?

"It's good to see you, Garrett." Wallace offered his hand. Clara felt relief when Garrett eyed him, shook, and offered a slight grin. Pride soared through her at Wallace's action. Papa filled in the gap when awkward silence threatened. "Supper's ready." Henry chided. "Dinner. I was told by my wife this is dinner 'cause supper is consumed in the kitchen."

How odd that the last time she ate in this room with family, Garrett had been present. Clara felt as though her search for an adventure had found its way back home.

"How's Mary, and everybody? I miss 'em."

"I've got a letter for you, by the way. And Porter assured me he'd check on my ladies while I'm away." He laughed. "Never mind that Cibby and George are next door."

"Who's Porter?" Pony James inquired. Mary's love interest was described to everyone. Clara smiled. Her friend would be proud of how Garrett spoke of Porter Franklin.

"You said business, is everything okay?"

"Business is good, Henry. I was here to finalize a sell."

Clara felt a slight heaviness settle in the room. Was Garrett needing to sell out the store or motel like Walter needed to sell the garage?

"Forgive me. I meant a purchase." Garrett looked at Ben, and Clara noted Papa's nod.

"It seems I'm the proud owner of Myer's Garage."

Clara's fork clinked against her plate. Wallace pushed back in his chair.

"You bought the garage?"

"I did, Wallace. It's now part of the Forder Empire, as I hear folks call it." Garrett cleared his throat. "I'd rename it Wallace's Garage if you're interested in staying in Layton."

Clara gasped, as did various others. However, Clara noted that Momma, Lena, and Papa showed no surprise on their faces. She'd call the expression joy.

Wallace squeezed her hand and laughed. "Let me ask my future wife if she'd like to stay."

"Yes!"

Lena applauded and was joined by the others.

"Truth is, Wallace, I got a business plan to propose for selling it to you over time. We can talk about that later."

Clara's head spun with the change of events. Garrett's generosity had not stopped with the garage. He also purchased the lot next to the garage for Jones Autos. Henry Jones would have his auto store. "After all, autos are becoming more necessary," Garrett had reasoned, "and folks around here can't often afford a new auto." Garrett had another purchase proposal to present Henry who suggested he'd call the place J & J Autos since most the cars would be repaired at Wallace James' garage.

While the Rain Whispered

Clara reckoned some folks may think her family was in bondage to the Forders. Truth was they deserved a heap of gratitude and hard work from her kin, but that wasn't shallow servitude. It was the give and take of friendship with deep roots.

Wallace and Clara James, she blushed at the name, would dwell in Layton, Texas, near the people with whom they'd breathed life, and even those gone before them nestled among the crepe myrtles. Her mind drifted to the first time Papa had hoisted her atop his shoulders and galloped around the yard when the butterflies danced. She'd not known such joy existed. She laced her fingers with Wallace's thick, masculine ones. Anticipation surged through her. Life was a gift from God who had abundant joy to offer.

An adventure.

Chapter 25
NOVEMBER & DECEMBER 1937 | LAYTON, TEXAS

A week from today was Thanksgiving. The weekend after that Clara would become Mrs. Wallace James. The groom-to-be marked up today's date on the wall calendar in his kitchen. "Her kitchen." Wallace laughed at his own words and ran a hand over a smooth chin. The beard was gone. It felt good to be himself again. In heart. In hope. In happiness. Oh, and in looks.

He touched the small flower he'd drawn over the word "shower" on today's date. Yep. He'd risked his manhood and drawn a flower. Clara had noted the date of every planned or special moment leading to their wedding day. "This calendar is our keepsake," she declared to him the day he hung it on the nail in the wall. "You're my keepsake," he'd declared in return, caring less that Wallace-with-no-beard had become rather sappy. He had leaned down to kiss Clara just as Maggie Carlson walked into the kitchen carrying a tablecloth. He'd managed to pull back in time, but hadn't forgotten that Maggie cost him a kiss.

In truth, he'd been happy to have Maggie with them that day as Clara began turning the home from his to theirs. A few days after Clara's arrival in Layton Maggie set out to redeem herself with them through an apology, not realizing she was already forgiven by them both. That's not to say the conversation was easy. There had been nothing flippant about the embarrassment over her actions toward him. Maggie and the interim, Graham, remained smitten with one another, and "a perfect fit" in Clara's own words. The four of them realized what Maggie had considered love for Wallace had been misplaced infatuation for an ideal. An ideal named Graham.

Wallace lifted the November calendar page and gazed at the words inscribed on December 4, 1937. "Wedding Day. Our adventure begins." The following week had "Honeymoon Adventure" spread across each date. The words evoked desire. Allowing his imagination to go outside the boundaries propriety had demanded, his senses felt her lying next to him, smelling her perfume, fingering enticing, short russet curls against his bare chest. He sucked in a breath.

They'd not be traveling for a honeymoon. He'd offered.

"Would you want to visit the beach at Galveston? Or travel to St. Louis? How about exploring New Orleans?"

"I want to explore us." The words hit his ears. He had to sit. *"And I can't think of a better place for our adventure to begin than in our home."*

"Not even a night in Dallas?" His response was weightless. A simple courtesy. A slight clarification.

"Nope."

Once 1937 became 1938, Wallace would be taking his bride to Austin so she could deliver her manuscript to Porterhouse Publishers. The plans were in place. Wallace moved to the front room and picked up the framed picture of he and Clara. Porter Franklin had come to town two weeks ago and taken the photograph. Days later, Mary presented it to them in a gold frame as an engagement present.

The clock struck eleven. Wallace darted back into the kitchen, braced himself and lifted a bulky box from the table. Katherine's creative wrapping was pleasing to the eye. He'd need to get his present to the Forder's home before ladies began arriving for the bridal luncheon. If he timed things just right, he might get a glimpse of his bride unnoticed. Nope. His automobile in the drive would announce his presence.

Would Clara be disappointed in such a practical gift—a typewriter—from her future husband? He had already paid Celeste, Ben's secretary, to give Clara typing lessons once the honeymoon was a precious memory. He whistled. No need to worry. The woman he loved would understand his hidden message. Wallace stole a glance at his bare wrist and smiled.

He rested his other arm on the package as he drove to the Forders. Sunshine warmed him and made the wildflowers pop along the roadside.

Clara passed the box of towels to Mary then smoothed the wrinkles in her satin fabric. The yellow dress with white and blue florals wrapped the blushing bride in sunshine and bluebonnets. She had never felt more lovely and loved. Emotion captured any eloquent words she might have spoken to the ladies surrounding her. Each one woven into the story of Clara and Wallace.

"Thank you all for the gifts." She paused. "I am more grateful than I can express." Momma and Aunt Lena rose from the green velvet couch next to the Forder's large fireplace. "There's one more present." Aunt Lena's wink caused a giggle through the guests. Oh, goodness! Surely Aunt Lena and Momma, of all people, wouldn't give her an embarrassing wedding night gown in front of people who had known her since she ran around in overalls. And...Wallace's Ma. She swallowed to suppress a hiccup.

The two returned carrying a present between them. Clara gasped. Her grandmother's small quilt was wrapped around a box and tied with a blue ribbon. The pastel patched quilt held a story Clara knew well. Though her grandmother had died long before Momma met Papa, she had told Katherine the quilt was an heirloom from her own mother. It was meant to adorn the foot of the newlywed bed for the first year of marriage. Clara had seen the quilt appear on Momma's bed after Papa returned home. She understood now that they must have felt like newlyweds again. Clara's little girl fingers had helped Aunt Lena place it on her own newlywed bed. The heirloom had spent more of its life in a trunk than on a bed as it awaited the next bride in the family.

Mrs. Forder pushed aside some small china cups and saucers on the coffee table. "Set it here." When the present rested on the table, Momma extended her hand to Clara. "It's too bulky for your lap." Clara rose and with no warning pulled Momma into a hug and reached for Lena at the same time. "I'm going to be a wife." The bride felt her Momma's smile against her shoulder. "Yes. Papa's Little Butterfly, my baby girl is getting married." Clara released the hug. Aunt Lena kissed her on the cheek then announced, "And Wallace is one excited man. It's about time he gets married and has him a newlywed bed." The loudest laugh came from Ella James. Heat surged through Clara from head to toe.

When the laughter settled, Clara bent down and pulled the blue ribbon loose from the quilt, then pulled each fold away to reveal a box embossed with the word "Royal." Clara's hands flew to her cheeks, and she stepped back. "Is this what I think it is?" Momma laughed. "Open it and see." At that moment

While the Rain Whispered

Clara noticed an envelope taped to the side of the box. Her name was written across the front. She knew that handwriting. The gift was from him.

"Wallace."

She slid her finger under the seal, loosened it, and retrieved a small slip of paper. Laughter escaped her. Wallace had typed a note with no capital letters. No doubt, he'd used one finger.

angels kissed her my heart stirred she called me friend i wanted her hope slipped away but returned as love our own story has just begun may these keys keep up with your stories my darling clara i love you

Tears fell on the box as she opened it then unlatched the case. "Oh, my." Her hands flew to her lips. She caught her breath. A shiny black typewriter smiled back at her, and nestled in the case lay Wallace's watch. Time and tools. He wanted his wife to write.

For this moment no one in the room mattered. She felt the keys then begin to press. Each key landed against an empty carriage, the chick-chick-cha-chick sounding out an opening line.

i l o v e w a l l a c e

———————◆•◆•◆———————

No one warned him he'd be struck speechless. Wallace slid his hand into the pants pocket of his new blue suit and fidgeted with the gold bands. His feet shifted, needing an outlet for his adrenaline. He hoped he wouldn't become a blubbering sap in front of the guests.

Then again, he hoped he would. Their world could see how overcome he was with love for his Clara.

Sheer net overlay the white satin fabric that puddled at her feet. His eyes grazed the length of his bride. Her slender shoulders enhanced the feminine gathers that draped them, while giving deference to the modest tease in the dipping neckline. A thin veil extending from a floral crown covered her face, adding to the mystique of this woman who was soon to be his. To love. To touch. To shelter. To treasure.

Her smile was unmistakable, and led him to her focus on her eyes. Not once did they glance from one another until her Papa lifted the veil and pressed his lips against the Little Butterfly's angel kiss. Ben caught his eye, and said a thousand things without words. Wallace nodded, then took the hand of his bride and slipped it through his arm. Her fingers moved back and forth over the fabric of his coat.

"You are so beautiful." The words floated from him to her. She winked. "I feel quite adventurous today." The whisper made his ears ring. "Me too."

———————◆—————

Clara nestled against him in the seat, his free arm pulling her into him, the other on the steering wheel. He beeped the auto, and the newlyweds waved to well-wishers as he sped away from the Forder house. He reckoned while standing in the foyer of the Forder home, he'd shaken the hand of every guest at the reception. He reckoned the cake tasted delicious. He reckoned Porter Franklin had taken every photograph Clara had asked for. He reckoned Willy, and Henry, and Mary, and Maggie had said nice things about them when asked to congratulate the happy couple. He reckoned. He reckoned. He reckoned. The only thing he'd known for sure was each move his bride had made. Every breath she took, every glance and touch between them as they mingled.

A gentle mist fell on the windshield as he pulled onto the gravel drive of their home. He eased his frame from the car. "Let's get you inside, Mrs. James, before it rains." His urgency was halted when he bent to kiss her, and he felt her linger in the moment until the mist gained momentum. Wallace scooped his bride into his arms, closed the door with his foot, then secured the hem of her wedding gown before hustling to the porch.

Her hand around his neck pulled his face toward hers. She kissed him. When he parted, his lips pressed against her ear. "Welcome home." Her lips found his neck. His pulse increased, so much more awaited them beyond the threshold.

He glanced around the front room, aware of the potpourri scent she favored, and kept moving toward the bedroom. He pulled the newlywed quilt to the floor and settled them on the bed, his lap filled with the beautiful woman kissed by an angel. He kissed each painted nail on her left hand, then pressed his lips against her mark. She sighed.

And while the rain whispered, he made her his wife.

Chapter 26

OCTOBER 1938 | LAYTON, TEXAS

Clara stood from the chair and stretched. Her lower back ached from hours of sitting at the kitchen table. She reckoned she'd become quite proficient at the typewriter and should be right proud. Wallace entered from the back door and wiped his brow with a handkerchief.

She loved Saturday evenings at home, knowing the next morning the alarm wouldn't ring until eight o'clock. Most times they woke before that time. Her husband would hold her, and what not, until their stomachs growled for attention.

Her lips pressed his slightly when she paused on her way to the icebox. "The sweet tea is nice and cold." As she handed him the chilly glass, he pulled her to him. "How's the story coming along?" She looked up and wiggled her fingers in front of him. "The words are flying out." He clasped some fingers and kissed them. "And how's the little one?" His hand moved to her rounded middle. She thread her fingers with his. "Little one has been kicking me the last hour. I reckon day and night doesn't matter." Wallace took a sip of tea. "Got his Momma's spunk." Clara wrinkled her nose. "I hope he or she doesn't." Wallace patted her head. "I hope he or she does."

An auto beeped outside. "Sounds like someone's here." Wallace mumbled as he darted to the sink and splashed water on his face. He grabbed the dish towel ran it across his cheeks. Clara hoisted her hands to her hips. "Oops." How many times had she told him the dish towel was for dishes? He folded it back onto the counter with deliberate motion and ceremony, then headed to the door. Clara straightened the papers on the table and closed the typewriter. Maybe Jacob and Raymond were coming by to play cards. And eat all the cookies she'd made this morning. Maybe it was the wrong house. Either way a pot of coffee was in order. She moved to the stove just as Wallace announced their guest.

Clara grabbed the counter in surprise then bounced on her feet. "Little One" joined in the excitement with a kick. She bounded to the front room.

Porter Franklin stood in the doorway, clasping the hand of his fiancée, Mary. In his other hand he held a book. *My book?*

"Hope you don't mind us dropping in unannounced." Porter motioned Mary into the room as he spoke. Clara noted his wide grin. Wallace chuckled. "Not at all. Have a seat." Thank goodness Wallace could form words. Clara couldn't.

No one sat. They all four formed a circle as Porter placed the book in Clara's hands. "Would you autograph this for me?"

Her fingers trembled. She ran her hand over the cover. How beautiful. "Windy Hop Tales by Clara James." She squealed. "And, Wallace, look. 'Illustrated by Lena Jones.'" His hug lifted her to his height. Her laughter filled the air. "Porter, this is perfect. More than I dreamed." Tears rolled down her cheeks of their own free will. "I. I don't know how to thank you."

Mary waved her hands in front of her face and squealed. "I told you you'd be a famous author." The women hugged. Clara's roundness met Mary's thin frame. Her friend pulled away and rubbed Clara's forearms. "Not much longer." She smiled. Clara pulled the book from her chest and rested a hand on belly. "Just enough time to be quite large at your wedding." They giggled.

Wallace reached for the book. "May I?" His grin threatened what bit of composure she had, so intense was her joy. "Let's sit and look together." Just as they sat on the couch, gravel popped in the driveway. Again. And again. And again. Porter's raised eyebrow toward Mary didn't go unnoticed. Clara pulled the curtain back on the window behind her.

"Why it's …well…every Jones, Williams, and James we call kin, and the Carlsons, and our new Reverend Graham, and…." She glanced at Mary. "The Forders." Her face turned to Wallace with wrinkled brows. What was this man up to? He leaned toward the window in exaggerated motion and shrugged. "And, looks like they're carrying food. Good. I'm hungry."

Wallace stood. Porter opened the door. Aunt Lena was the first inside, her hands oddly empty while the other women each carried a dish. Uncle Henry came in behind her, handsome and well. His eyes shone; his smile was unforced. Clara's heart stirred. It was good to have him back in the light.

Clara caught on to the moment, and cast her husband a smile. She placed the book behind her.

"Aunt Lena, what's going on?"

"I most certainly don't know." She raised her hands in the air. "Just as I was fixin' supper, Henry came in and put away the food. Drug me to the auto and said he was taking me to eat. And here I am." She slung her arm toward the front yard. "With a whole parade and dinner on the ground following me." She leaned into Henry and sucked in a deep breath. "Doesn't make sense."

"It makes perfect sense." Clara pulled the book from behind her back and handed it to Lena.

"Windy Hop Tales." Lena gasped, turned to Henry, then back again.

Joy was written all over Lena's face.

Clara's own joy formed into laughter and filled the room.

Words weren't necessary.

Author Notes

The Letters to Layton series was birthed by love for my grandmother and a strong desire to give her what life never did. It has grown into a love for the characters who began as shadows of real people but transformed into their own beings. Thank you for sharing their story with me.

My family faced our fair amount of trials over the time it took to write this story. Wonderful moments were sprinkled in between the tough ones. Such is life. I thank God for His peace during trying times. I wish for every reader to know Jesus personally and experience that same peace for now and eternity.

Special thanks to my ministry colleague and Georgia State Senator, Wes Cantrell, for letting me brainstorm some ideas with him on the inner workings of state government and for explaining complicated jargon to a lay person.

A special congratulations to Connie Porter Saunders for participating in a Facebook Party and supplying me the character name Porter Franklin. I like his character. Thank you to Lana Lynne Higginbotham for her Facebook participation and offering the name Windy Hop Tales for Clara's stories. She has graciously relinquished the whimsical title to this series and any further works. I deeply appreciate Madie Morton and her family allowing me to use her beautiful first name for sweet Madie Forder. Suzanne Slayton kindly allowed me to use her last name for the villain. Cass McKenna, I was struck by the sound of your name when I met you at your family's home in San Antonio. My sister Monica, your daughter-in-law, thought you wouldn't mind if I borrowed your first name and let it be a surprise.

To other friends and family who may have recognized a first or last name scattered here or there, I was happy when it came to mind and fit the scene or character. I hope you are as well. For all other intents, any full names belonging to real people were unintentional and coincidental.

Thank you to my friend Mavi for her always-well-timed encouragement. My beta readers, Michelle and Anatasia, offered valuable input. I cannot fully express my appreciation for their time. The story became richer and deeper because of them. Thank you both. Hats-off to my ACFW Chapter for your input.

Thank you to my husband, Lynn, who took me to San Antonio, Fredericksburg, and Austin to explore the setting first hand. Our time there added to my childhood memories of visiting those locations. Not only did he spend hours traveling with me, he also allowed me many hours closed off in my office to write and rewrite. My family are the ones who prompted me to tell my stories. The best way to express how they make me feel is to quote my toddler grandson, "Wow."

To my readers, I am humbled by your support and encouragement. When the writing got tough, one of you seemed to always speak or write a word of encouragement or anticipation. Those comments kept my fingers on the keyboard. An unloved story is a sad thing. Thanks for loving my stories.

To my Savior and Heavenly Father, thank you for continually teaching me more about who you are and loving me when I doubt, pout, worry, fuss, or mess up. I want my life and my words to honor and glorify you.

———◆•◆•◆———

Many have asked how true to life are the three books in this series. I'm happy to share that with you if you choose to read further. For the sake of clarity, I'll use the character names as I separate fact and fiction.

Katherine McGinn Williams: She is based on my maternal great grandmother. She did marry Ben Williams and give birth to Clara. However, whatever happened that sent Ben away was not passed down to the generations. They never reunited. Katherine lived in a house with her sister and two brothers who worked the railroad for a while. She was the only one of them to marry, though she and Ben lived together less than a year. They met through her brother, Joe. In a census when Clara was ten-years-old, she listed herself as widowed, but records indicate that Ben lived many years beyond that census.

Ben Williams: The character is based on my great grandfather whose last name really was Williams. Before he met Katherine, Ben had been married.

He had a son and a set of boy and girl twins with his wife. Sadly, records show that the twin son died as a young infant and months later so did his first wife. There is no indication that Katherine knew of his children. Perhaps that was the issue between them. The letters that Ben wrote, which inspired the writing of this series, indicate that he worked the railroad, and that at the time of writing them, he did not know if his child with Katherine was a boy or girl. He begged to be reunited with Katherine and the baby. Years later, Ben died as the result of an auto accident.

Clara: Based on my maternal grandmother, Clara grew up in the house with her mother, aunt, and two uncles. Indications are that one of the uncles mistreated Clara. According to a family history book she filled out, Clara never knew her father and wondered about him as a girl. She was born "in a veil" as written into *Among the Crepe Myrtles*. My grandmother recalls working the cotton fields with her mother. Clara did marry Wallace. He was one of nine children. They met at a brush arbor meeting when she was a teenager. Katherine attended every date he took her own. They married against her wishes in a barn on a turkey farm. Eventually Clara was in the good graces of her mother again. Clara and Wallace had four children. Sadly, one was stillborn and one had cerebral palsy. My mom and her sister were their only children to live into adulthood. Clara and Wallace lived next door to Katherine and her siblings. Clara was a homemaker. They lived humbly and struggled to make every cent count. Clara was not a writer, but thought she might have enjoyed being a teacher.

Lena: Based on Katherine's sister, she is my great aunt. Lena never married and died a spinster. I remember her sitting in her rocker chewing and spitting snuff. I make Lena a good cook and Katherine a poor one in the stories. The truth is most of the women through this family line are good Southern cooks and make delicious sweet tea. I used to call my Mom "the bestest cooker." I hope I didn't break the chain.

Henry: Henry, along with most the other characters in the books, is fictitious. I enjoyed getting to know him and giving Lena a happy life.

Layton: based on the small town of Lavon, Texas.

Miscellaneous: Many items in the books are based on real heirlooms— the clock, the rockers, Clara's tea set, the ring Ben gives to Katherine, and items on the covers of the first two books to name a few. The butterfly book is part of my imagination.

As for the angel kiss, my grandmother had a brown mark on her cheek. Though no one called it an angel kiss, I wanted to give it that special name in my stories.

Truth can be stranger than fiction, and such is the case for the real people on whom I based this series. It has been my honor to share bits and pieces of fact with fiction and give my grandparents a little of what life didn't offer them.

I would love to stay in touch with you.

Email: *kimwilliamsbook@gmail.com*

Website: *www.kimwilliamsbook.wordpress.com*

Facebook: *https://www.facebook.com/kimwilliamsbook/*

Twitter: *https://twitter.com/KimWlm*

Pinterest: *https://www.pinterest.com/kimwilliams0903/*

Made in the USA
Coppell, TX
06 November 2019